A WEDDING ON SUNFLOWER STREET

AN UPLIFTING STORY ABOUT FRIENDSHIP, LOVE AND MARRIAGE

SUNFLOWER STREET
BOOK FIVE

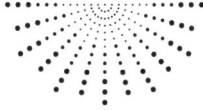

RACHEL GRIFFITHS

COSY COTTAGE BOOKS

For my family, with love always. XXX

A WEDDING ON SUNFLOWER STREET

Summer has come to Sunflower Street and there's excitement in the air …

Lila Edwards is enjoying her pregnancy and counting down the days until her June wedding. Lila's fiancé, Ethan Morris, has decorated the nursery, and everything seems to be going to plan until an unexpected visitor arrives in the village.

Roxie and Fletcher Walker are enjoying the summer with their two dogs and Roxie is busier than ever helping Lila with her wedding plans. Roxie is determined to ensure that Lila and Ethan have a wonderful day.

Joanne Baker and Max Jenkins have moved in together and are making the most of lazy weekends and country walks. They're keeping an eye on the property market but nothing they've seen is quite right. If only they could find the perfect home to make their own.

Join the residents of Sunflower Street as they prepare for the wedding of the year, discover a long-hidden secret and look forward to a new arrival.

1

LILA AND ETHAN

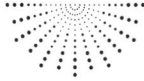

*I*t's the most beautiful place I've ever seen.' Lila said as she closed the car door and looked around. 'I mean, I know I've been here before, when I picked up wine from the shop, but I'd forgotten just how lovely it is.'

'It's pretty special, isn't it?' Ethan wrapped an arm around her shoulders, and she leaned into him.

'It's just perfect,' Roxie Walker nodded. 'I can see it all now … a perfect June day, the sun high in the sky, the birds singing, a gentle breeze toying with your veil.'

They had come to the Chester-Linden Vineyard to see the wedding venue there. So far, they'd only just got out of the car and they'd been overwhelmed by the beauty of the landscape. Lila had asked Roxie to accompany them in case she needed a second opinion, and also because Roxie was her closest friend and Lila wanted to know what she thought of the place too. Roxie had offered to help with the wedding planning and Lila was glad to have her support because making so many decisions was daunting and she knew that

Ethan would just go along with whatever she wanted. Roxie's critical eye would help Lila avoid making any mistakes.

The thirty-five-minute drive from Wisteria Hollow had taken them through green-hedged country lanes where the scents of fields and hedgerows permeated the air, sweet and floral, rich and peaty. As they'd crested a small hill, the patch-work of fields had spread out before them, green and gold, fresh and fertile. There was so much beauty on their doorstep and Lila would never tire of getting outside and enjoying the sights and sounds.

Ethan had slowed the car when they spotted the sign for the vineyard then he'd taken a left turn and driven along a narrow lane that ended in a gravel car park. From there they could see the large manor house where the Chester-Linden family had lived for generations. The house and estate had an 800-year history and Ethan had been excited when he'd discovered that, reading the information from the website to Lila. The vineyard that had been planted in 1979 occupied a gently sloping four-hectare site adjacent to the house. The winery buildings and shop were off to the far left of the house, while opposite it was the wedding venue itself, a large barn that had been extended and renovated recently to cater for weddings, parties, barn dances and more. When Lila had visited the shop some time ago, the barn had been in the very early stages of a renovation, so she was keen to see the finished changes.

There were three other cars in the car park and Lila wondered if they belonged to other couples planning to get married there. She'd gone through a roller-coaster of emotions as she and Ethan had discussed where they'd like to say their vows. The village church in Wisteria Hollow had initially been disregarded because it was where Lila had been due to marry Ben the Bastard, but then she'd thought that wouldn't matter as it was in the past. However, when they'd gone to speak to the vicar after Christmas in order to test the waters, Lila had started to shake and she'd known that she couldn't get married there. The place held far too many unpleasant memories of the day Ben had failed to show, of how her heart had raced and her knees had threatened to give way beneath her as reality washed over her like an ice-cold wave. Ethan had been wonderfully understanding and they'd embarked upon a search for the perfect venue, but each one had either been fully booked for the foreseeable future or just not right.

When Ethan had seen an online advert for the barn renovation at the Chester-Linden Vineyard, something inside Lila had lifted. The website had shown a venue that was everything she could have wanted and more. She'd tried to caution herself against getting her hopes up, but her belly was getting bigger by the day and she was aware that if they didn't find somewhere soon, she'd have to resign herself to waiting until after their baby was born. That would have been fine too, but Lila liked the idea of being married before their baby came along, something she knew was linked to her own need for security after her difficult childhood. Besides which, she was a bit afraid that if they delayed the wedding, they'd be too busy and they might not get around to it for months or possibly years because the baby would be their priority.

'What if those other cars belong to people who want to book their wedding here too?' Lila asked as they made their way across the car park in the direction of the barn.

'It doesn't matter,' Ethan said, holding her hand tight. 'I'm sure lots of people will want to get married here when they see how lovely it is.'

'Yes but there might not be any availability in June or July and then we'll have to wait.'

Ethan stopped walking and turned her to face him.

'If we have to wait, we can wait, but I have a feeling that the first Saturday in June will be free.'

'You do?' Lila looked into his brown eyes, noted the smile playing on his lips. 'How do you know that?'

He winked. 'I might just have secured it as soon as we saw the website.'

'But how?' Roxie was standing next to them, her head cocked on one side. 'I'd have thought this place would've been booked up months in advance.'

'It was.' Ethan nodded. 'But there was a cancellation and I swooped in and paid a deposit immediately.'

'So we *can* get married here?' Lila gasped.

'We can. As long as you like the inside of the barn too. I mean, it's perfect out here for photographs, but we need to ensure that you like where the ceremony will take place too.'

'I can't wait to see it.' Lila tugged at his hand.

'It looked wonderful online,' Roxie said.

'I'm hoping it will be even better in person.' Ethan grinned, raising Lila's hand and kissing it. 'Now let's go and meet the wedding planner.'

∽

ETHAN'S HEART was brimming as they walked towards the barn. He'd known as soon as he'd seen the venue that it would be perfect and that Lila would love it. He thought it was better than a church. He understood why people wanted to get married in churches but he wasn't religious and had liked the idea of a different kind of venue. With Lila being pregnant, he hadn't wanted to suggest going abroad – although it would have been a possibility – and they'd been busy decorating the nursery and getting things ready for the baby's arrival. Staying close to home seemed like a better idea, and he hoped it would be a bit cheaper too. The fact that the vineyard had a cancellation for just five weeks' time had meant that he was able to barter for a lower price, and the fact that their guest list was small, meant that he'd got a very good deal. His mum had insisted on helping out and so, as long as Lila approved of the venue, everything was good to go.

Outside the barn, they stopped and looked around. A tall woman in a lilac suit with short black hair was striding towards them, a clipboard tucked under one arm. Ethan recognised her from her photo on the website.

'That's Cesca Howes, the wedding planner.'

'She was on the website,' Roxie said. 'She seems taller in real life.'

'Hello! Hello!' Cesca reached them, bringing with her the scent of expensive perfume and a perfectly white smile. 'So good to meet you.'

She shook their hands firmly then balanced the clipboard on her hip. 'So this is for the Edwards-Morris wedding?'

'That's right,' Ethan replied.

'And you wanted the first Saturday in June?'

'Right again.'

'Wonderful!' Cesca smiled. 'I just had to double-check because there'd be nothing worse than getting the date wrong. Or the names of the groom or bride confused.'

She looked at Roxie. 'Are you the bride's mum?'

Roxie coughed then laughed. 'Well—'

'This is my friend, Roxie Walker,' Lila interrupted.

'I thought you looked far too young to be her mum. But hey-ho, I'm terrible at judging ages and these days people often look so good it's hard to tell if they're thirty or fifty.' Cesca shrugged then gave a long sigh. 'Huge apologies for my faux pas, Ms Walker.'

'It's not a problem,' Roxie smiled. 'I like to think of myself as a kind of foster mum to Lila anyway.'

'Wonderful!' Cesca made a note on her clipboard. 'Will anyone else be joining us this morning? Mums or dads? Grandparents? Other family members?'

Lila and Ethan shook their heads and Ethan's stomach plummeted. He had hoped that these subjects wouldn't be raised but then Cesca was probably used to greeting bride and groom, or bride and bride, or groom and groom, along with extended family, and so wanted to ensure that everyone was included.

'It's just us three today,' he said, keen to clarify before Cesca asked anything else.

'Wonderful.' She nodded, making Ethan wonder if everything in Cesca's life was wonderful. 'Let's show you around then, shall we?'

Cesca opened the door to the barn and stepped aside, gesturing for them to go in.

~

THE INTERIOR of the barn was cool and smelt like a summer meadow; the sweetness of roses was combined with the honey-mint of freesias. Lila realised it was due to the beautiful flower arrangements on stands either side of the doorway.

Ethan took her hand as they walked further into the barn and looked around. The ceiling was high and skylights had been set above the exposed beams, letting in plenty of light. Their footsteps echoed on the polished wooden floorboards and Lila felt Roxie take her free arm and squeeze it. Around the edges of the barn were narrow tables and benches in different colours including pink, blue and green. They were clearly upcycled and gave the barn a shabby chic feel. Each table had three colourful glass votive holders along the middle with heart cut-outs and Lila could imagine how they would look with candles burning inside, casting flickering hearts across the tables. Dried flowers were wrapped around the ceiling beams and in between them, tiny lights twinkled; something that would no doubt look even better as darkness fell outside.

'We could set the aisle up along here with chairs either side. Well, actually you can have chairs, benches or hay bales.' Cesca pointed at the centre of the wooden floor. 'And you could have the desk with the registrar at the end there.' On the opposite side of the room were glass bifold doors. 'The doors can be open or closed and, as you can see, they have a wonderful view of the fields beyond.'

'Hay bales?' Lila asked, imagining the smell of hay filling the barn then picturing some of the guests complaining about the effect it would have on their clothes. It would be difficult to please everyone and that was another reason why she was glad they'd opted for a small wedding.

'We've had special requests since we opened as a wedding venue.' Cesca nodded. 'So added it to our list.'

'Surely hay would destroy a silk dress?' Roxie asked, ever the fashionista.

'We can cover the top of the bales with cushions,' Cesca explained. 'It's more for the authentic barn effect and believe me, it would smell magnificent.'

'I can imagine.' Ethan smiled at Lila, his eyes bright. He was clearly pleased with his choice.

'If you want a band, we can organise that too, whether you want a covers band, string band, harpist or something else. This could be for during the ceremony and afterwards as well if you intend on having the reception here too, which we are hoping you are. There's a space in the corner to the left of the doors where we can set up a raised area for the band. While you all have photos done, the barn can be rearranged for the reception and, weather permitting, guests can enjoy some time outside with Pimm's or our own sparkling rosé or a combination. There are many possibilities, so today I want to check that you like what you see and then we can get to work on your list of wants.'

Lila nodded. 'It sounds perfect.'

'Why don't we have a sit down and I'll send for some refreshments then we can start planning?' Cesca gestured at a table near the door so they headed over to it and sat down, Cesca on one side, Lila flanked by Ethan and Roxie on the other.

'Do you mind if I take some photos?' Roxie asked. 'So we can show them to Lila's friends.'

'Of course not. Carry on.' Cesca smiled then turned over the page on her clipboard and looked at Lila and Ethan. 'Okay then you two. Let's get some ideas down.'

Half an hour later, Lila felt like they were getting somewhere. Following a quick text from Cesca, a young man wearing a white apron had arrived with a tray of tea and cake. They'd eaten the lemon drizzle cake and drunk the Earl Grey tea as Cesca had talked them through the options available.

'It feels real now,' Ethan said.

'It does.' Lila felt almost breathless as everything whirled around inside her mind.

'It's very exciting, isn't it?' Cesca smiled. 'I'm sure you'll have a wonderful day. Regarding that … will you be walking along the aisle alone, Lila, or do you have someone to walk with you? Traditionally, of course, we'd ask if you have someone to *give you away* but I like to think that's a bit old-fashioned now. However, it is nice to have someone to hold your hand as you walk towards your future spouse.'

Cesca waited, pen poised above the paper, and Lila opened and closed her mouth. Of course Lila should have thought about this, but it was one of those things she'd pushed away. She had decided that she wouldn't be inviting her parents not long after Ethan had proposed. What would be the point? They'd have some excuse not to come or they'd turn up and ruin the wedding in some way. They were like strangers to her now and she didn't want to ruin the day by worrying about what they might say or do, about the tension that having them there would cause.

'I'll do it.' Roxie spoke quietly. 'If you'd like me to, that is.'

Lila looked at her friend and her throat tightened. 'Really?'

'Of course. I don't see it as giving you away though, like Cesca said. It's more about being there with you, showing you off and supporting you.'

'Thank you so much.'

'It'll be my pleasure, Lila.'

'How lovely!' Cesca made a note on her clipboard. 'Have you got the dress yet?' Her eyes roamed over Lila.

'Not yet.' Lila placed a hand on her tummy. 'I wasn't sure how big I'd be.'

Cesca tilted her head. 'Do you mind me asking how far along you are?'

'About six months.'

'Really? But you're tiny. My sister was enormous at five months. You have the neatest little bump. It's just adorable.'

'Thank you.' Lila's cheeks were warm. 'I feel like a hippo.'

'That's because you're so tiny usually.' Roxie gently nudged Lila.

'As I keep telling you, Lila, you're keeping our baby warm and I don't think you've ever looked more beautiful.'

Ethan leant over and gave Lila a kiss and she relaxed against him. How could she be so lucky? For months now, she'd been waiting for something to happen, for something to go wrong and prove that she wasn't entitled to be happy and to have things to look forward to, but so far, it hadn't happened. She regularly pinched herself to ensure that she was awake and not deep in a beautiful dream.

'You are just the sweetest couple and I can't wait to see you on your wedding day all dressed up, glowing and happy.'

Cesca clapped her hands. 'Okay, folks, I think I have all I need for now. You have my number and email if you need anything else or have any questions. I'll send you the sample meal and buffet menus as well as the cake menu and we can sort all that out next week. Would you like to see outside now?'

'I'd love to.' Lila stood up carefully and Ethan held her hand while she stepped over the seat of the bench.

'Then I shall lead the way.'

Cesca marched towards the door, but before they left the barn, Lila and Ethan took one more look around. In just five weeks they'd be getting married here, making a commitment to each other in front of family and friends. The thought was at once exciting and terrifying, but Lila knew without a doubt that it was exactly what she wanted.

2

ROXIE

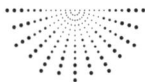

'This beef is delicious,' Joanne Baker pointed at her plate with her fork. Her cheeks were rosy, her green eyes bright. 'How'd you get it so tender?'

Roxie smiled. 'Don't cook it for too long.'

'She's right you know,' Fletcher said as he topped up everyone's glasses with red wine. 'Overcook it and it'll dry right up. Remember that first roast you made, Rox? Like a brick it was.'

Roxie shook her head. 'You cheeky sod. That was years ago and I was learning to cook.'

'It didn't take you long to get it right though, did it?' He winked at her.

'Not really, no. And then I taught you too so we can both make a tasty Sunday dinner.'

Joanne pushed a stray strand of ginger hair behind her ear. 'My parents make a good roast dinner but they often overcook the meat. Mum's paranoid about giving us all food poisoning so always adds an extra thirty minutes to whatever the instructions suggest as a guide. The chicken can be quite dry at times. Of course, I'd never tell them that though as they'd be devastated.'

'Your parents are too lovely to upset them.' Roxie nodded.

'These Yorkshire puddings are pretty amazing too,' Max Jenkins, Joanne's partner, said. 'How'd you get them to rise like that?'

'Use plain flour, not self-raising, and ensure the oil is *very* hot before pouring in the batter. Fletcher makes the Yorkshire puddings.' Roxie nodded at him. 'He's perfected the art.'

'I could easily eat two of these dinners,' Joanne said as she forked another roast potato into her mouth.

'Help yourself. There's plenty left.' Roxie offered the bowl of potatoes to her friend who helped herself then passed the bowl to Max.

'How did yesterday go?' Joanne asked.

'Really well. The venue at the vineyard is beautiful.' Roxie thought back to yesterday when she'd gone with Lila and Ethan to see the Chester-Linden Vineyard.

'Are they going to have the wedding there?' Joanne took a sip of wine.

'It looks like it. The date they've booked is five weeks yesterday.' Roxie nodded. 'As long as they have fine weather, it'll be perfect. After dinner I'll show you the photos on my phone.'

'It's a good choice. A friend of mine has booked it for August next year. I imagine it'll get pretty busy now.' Max pushed his square tortoiseshell glasses back up his nose.

'The wedding planner said they've got lots of bookings already. Lila and Ethan were very lucky to get a cancellation.'

'Not so lucky for the people who cancelled though.' Joanne grimaced. 'Poor things.'

Roxie saw Max reach across the table and squeeze Joanne's hand. They were such a sweet couple and looked very good together – Joanne with her pale skin and freckles and Max with his thick dark hair and brown eyes.

'If we'd waited, perhaps we could have renewed our vows there,' Fletcher said.

'I'm glad we did it here in our garden.' Roxie smiled. 'It was beautiful, intimate and exactly how I'd imagined it.'

Fletcher nodded. 'It was lovely.'

They had renewed their wedding vows in the spring with just Lila, Ethan, Joanne, Max and Roxie's parents present. It had been a quiet ceremony in their back garden and they'd celebrated with champagne and fish and chips afterwards.

Joanne frowned. 'Goodness, I've just realised that they don't have long to plan at all. What about a dress, and suit, and bridesmaids?'

'They don't have long but we can all help. Perhaps we should suggest dress shopping as a priority?'

Joanne nodded. 'Unless Lila decides to make the dress herself.'

'She certainly has the ability to make it. I'll phone her later and see what she's thinking. She was so overwhelmed by the excitement of seeing the venue yesterday that I didn't want to ask too many questions, but as time is of the essence, we'd better get on with it.'

'But first we need dessert,' Fletcher said, rising and taking their empty plates. 'Nothing should be done until after we've eaten some raspberry pavlova.'

'Sounds good to me.' Joanne grinned.

Roxie helped her husband with the plates, but her mind wasn't on meringues, raspberries and cream, it was on how she could help Lila to get everything organised with as little stress as possible.

~

LATER THAT AFTERNOON, Roxie and Fletcher sat on the wooden swing in their garden. The swing had been something they'd wanted for a while and had finally bought as a mutual treat. It had padded white seats and a white canopy and was extremely comfortable. Roxie had her feet on her husband's lap and he was pushing them gently each time his feet touched the decking.

'Look at those two.' Roxie pointed at their two dogs, Glenda the pug and Stinky, the Yorkipoo. Since they'd adopted Stinky at Christmas, Glenda had become very fond of her and the two dogs were now inseparable. They were currently roaming the grass together, sniffing everything, occasionally distracted by the butterflies that visited the flowers. Stinky had almost caught one but it flew off just in time.

'They're best friends now, aren't they?' Fletcher squeezed Roxie's foot. 'Are you still glad I said we'd have Stinky?'

'Of course I am. But that name … it's a shame we can't change it.' Roxie giggled. Stinky had been named by her previous owner and it seemed wrong to change her name now as she was used to it, but every time Roxie called her, it made her cringe.

'It kind of suits her, don't you think?' Fletcher raised his eyebrows. 'She does have rather bad flatulence.'

'It's not so bad now she's on the raw diet.'

'True.'

Roxie rested her head on the cushion of the seat and closed her eyes. The gentle breeze caressed her skin, toyed with her long black hair and carried the scent of the roses in their garden. She had a full belly after their Sunday dinner and felt completely relaxed. There was nothing better than spending time with her husband and dogs in their beautiful home.

'I forgot to tell you earlier,' Fletcher interrupted her thoughts. 'But when I went to the shop for the papers this morning, I think I saw Lila.'

Roxie opened her eyes. 'You think?'

'She was walking in the opposite direction but I'm sure it was her. Same blonde hair, same small frame. I called her name, but she carried on walking as if she hadn't heard me.'

'Did you call loudly?'

'No, but I didn't want to shout at her. I might have startled her as well as the gathering of grannies outside the shop.'

'Perhaps she didn't hear you.'

'I guess not. Either that or she didn't want to speak to me.' He pulled a face.

'She could have been lost in thoughts of her wedding. I wouldn't take it personally.'

'I won't. Just thought I'd tell you that's all.'

'And don't say *gathering of grannies*. They might not all be grandmothers, you know?'

He grinned. 'It was the lovely group of ladies who do the knitting for the premature baby unit at the hospital. And they are, to my knowledge, all grannies.'

Roxie shook her head. 'Charmed them all did you?'

Fletcher laughed.

'Just keep rubbing my feet like that, Fletcher, because it's really good and then I'll make you a beef and mustard sandwich for tea as a reward.'

'Yes, my dearest.' He gave a small salute. 'Whatever the lady wants, the lady gets. And a beef sandwich sounds perfect.'

Roxie closed her eyes and lay back, letting the peace of the afternoon soothe her, feeling incredibly grateful for their lovely home on Sunflower Street.

3

LILA

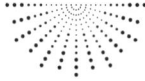

'There's so much to organise,' Lila flopped back against the sofa cushions and stared at the notepad on her lap in despair.

'It's not that bad,' Roxie took the notepad from Lila and looked at it. 'Priorities are a dress for you, suit for Ethan and flowers. Cesca said they'd sort the drinks and catering and anything else you want them to.'

Lila swallowed hard. 'It's not just that, though, Rox. I'm worried about money. I mean … we're getting the venue at a discount because of the cancellation but I don't want to go overboard with everything else. It's an important day but it's just one day out of our life together.'

'You're keeping the guest list small though, right?'

Lila nodded. 'Very small. Just fifty for the ceremony and reception and all from Wisteria Hollow.'

'I think small is better, sweetheart. It'll be more personal. People go mad about weddings and have hundreds there and it can become silly. Not that I'm criticising big weddings, because it's up to the individuals involved, but for you and Ethan I think this is right.'

'After last time as well … I just don't want to make it a huge event.' Lila shuddered as she thought of the money and planning that had gone into her first wedding; about the waste, about the horror of the humiliation when Ben had failed to show.

'I know you're thinking about last time, honey, but that isn't going to happen again. Ethan is not Ben.'

'I know that. He's not remotely like Ben. But we did waste money and time and you're right, I'd prefer to keep things more intimate now.'

'What about bridesmaids? Are you going to bother?'

'I don't think so. I mean … I know it's nice but there's only you and Joanne who I'd have chosen, and you said you'll walk me down the aisle and then it would just be Joanne and … well … do you think she'll understand if I don't?'

'Of course she will.' Roxie patted Lila's hand. 'She won't mind at all.'

'Okay then.' Lila exhaled slowly. 'So it's just a dress for me.'

'Do you want to go shopping? It can still be exciting.'

'I'm not sure, Roxie. As you know, I did all that last time with the big dress and the veil and the shoes and … they ended up in the greyhound rescue charity shop.'

'I know.' Roxie inclined her head. 'I insisted you take them there, remember?'

'I do. This time, I'd like something simpler. So yes, can we go shopping and have a look but preferably not in bridal shops?'

'Absolutely. When do you want to go?'

Lila placed a hand on her belly. 'I think the sooner the better to be honest, even if it's just to get some ideas because I haven't a clue. Although whatever I get will need to have some give in it because I could grow a lot bigger in five weeks.'

'You look wonderful.'

'Thanks. I feel like a beach ball.'

'You'll never look like a beach ball.'

Lila smiled at her friend then her eyes wandered over Roxie's trim figure in her yoga leggings and vest top, her shiny black hair in French plaits, her face flawlessly made-up. Roxie always looked immaculate. Usually, that wasn't a problem for Lila, but today, she felt frumpy in her baggy jogging bottoms and T-shirt.

'I don't feel like I look great, though, Rox. It's not the bump because I love the bump, but my bottom and thighs are growing too and nothing fits. And as for these.' She looked down at her ample chest.

'They're a fabulous addition.'

'They're tender and hard as rocks. I had no idea I was in for all this change. I know that sounds daft because I was aware that pregnancy changed a woman's body but I had no idea how much. Boobs, ass and thighs all have extra jiggle.' She snorted. 'It's not even funny really, but then it kind of is.'

'What matters is that you're fit and healthy and that the baby is fit and healthy. Your body will change, Lila, but it's all perfectly natural. You might not be able to see it but you're gorgeous.'

'I'm so glad you're here, Roxie.'

'Me too, darling.'

Roxie shuffled closer and they hugged and Lila relaxed into her friend's embrace. She felt like she could tell Roxie anything and not be judged. *Well, almost anything …*

When Roxie released her and sat back again, she pulled her phone from the pocket in her leggings. 'Shall I text Joanne and ask what day's good for her this week?'

'What day?' Lila asked.

'To go dress shopping?'

'Oh! Yes, of course. I can do any day. The bonus of being self-employed, right?'

Roxie typed a text to their friend then stood up. 'Time for tea and crumpets?'

'It is just gone eleven.'

'You stay there and put your feet up and I'll make our elevenses.'

'You spoil me.'

'That's what friends are for.'

Roxie sashayed out to the kitchen and Lila curled her legs up underneath her on the sofa. Within seconds, as if sensing that her mistress was relaxing, Cleocatra, Lila's ginger cat had jumped up next to her and snuggled into her feet like a warm, fluffy blanket.

'Hey Cleo. How're you today?' Lila ran a hand over Cleo's soft fur and the cat purred loudly. It was like a sedative, making Lila feel sleepy, so she lay down with her head on a cushion while Cleo climbed over her legs and cuddled into Lila's bump.

The warm cat, the sunshine pouring through the window and the sounds of Roxie tinkering around in the kitchen all soothed Lila and sent her into a peaceful doze.

∼

'HELLO YOU.' Lila smiled at Ethan as he entered the kitchen later that afternoon. 'How was your day?'

'Busy.' He nodded. 'But all the better for seeing you.'

She walked into his embrace and breathed him in, sighing as his strong arms encircled her, their baby nestled between them.

'How was your day?' he asked.

'Good. Roxie came round and we talked about wedding dresses and I had a doze, then we had elevenses followed by lunch then I snuggled up with Cleo and looked at some wedding magazines.'

'You're just catching up on your sleep, that's all. Did you see any dresses you liked?'

'No. I was looking for inspiration but I didn't find any.' She stepped back and looked at his handsome face. 'You look tired.'

'I'm okay. That renovation I've been working on for Bridget has turned out to be a bigger job than I first thought but Nina's proving to be quite capable.'

Nina Fry was Ethan's apprentice. She was only eighteen and had talked about going travelling at some point soon, but according to Ethan she was a good worker and he'd be sorry to lose her now.

'That's good to hear.'

Ethan had taken on a renovation project for the café owner Bridget Wibberley. Her elderly mother had passed away in the winter and rather than sell her mother's cottage, she'd decided to have it renovated first and asked Ethan to do the work. It was a big job but one that he was keen to accept, especially now that they had a baby on the way.

'She'll have added a significant sum to the cottage's value with all the work she's having done, and when it goes on the market I suspect there will be a long queue to view it.'

'That's exciting. I wonder if Joanne and Max will look at it.'

'I would think so. Bridget thinks a lot of Joanne, so she'll probably let her go and see it first.'

'I hope so.' Lila hugged him again, enjoying the security of being in his arms. 'Are you hungry?'

'You know me.'

'Hollow legs.' She laughed.

'Always.'

'What do you fancy for dinner?'

'Anything at all. I could pop out and get a takeaway if you fancy one?'

'I don't mind cooking. I have plenty in the fridge and besides which, you're exhausted so you need a hot bath and an early night.'

'I'm so rock and roll.' He rubbed his eyes and yawned.

'You and me both.' She ran a hand over her bump. 'But it's nice.'

'What is?'

'Being able to enjoy this time when it's just us and the cats.'

'I guess we should make the most of being able to sleep while we can, eh?'

'Definitely.'

'I'll go and run a bath then we can make dinner together.'

'You sure?'

'I am.' He walked to the door that led to the hallway then paused. 'Oh … I meant to say … Nina popped to the café today to get some coffees and she said she saw you crossing the road. She called to you but you carried on walking and she was worried she'd done something to offend you.'

'I didn't go out today, remember? Roxie came round.'

'Oh.' He knitted his brows. 'Perhaps it was just someone who looked like you.'

'Must have been. Anyway, I would never deliberately ignore someone, especially not Nina. Why would I do that?'

'I didn't think you would and I told her that. She just swore it was you.'

'That's really odd.' Lila shook her head. 'Who around here looks that much like me?'

'No one I know. Right … bath, food and an early night it is.'

Ethan left the kitchen and Lila went to the back door and opened it, letting the cool evening air into the room. She hated the thought that someone might think she'd ignored them. She was certain she hadn't been anywhere today other than the back garden but it made her wonder for a moment. Was she getting forgetful in her pregnancy? Had she gone out and forgotten about it?

She shook her head. Absolutely not. She'd been home all day and Roxie had been here for most of it. Nina was mistaken and that was all there was to it.

Just then, a meow from the garden caught her attention and she smiled as William Shakespaw ran towards her then twirled around her legs.

'Hello, Willy. Where've you been all day?' she asked the black and white cat. He peered up at her and blinked. 'Oh, I see … keeping it to yourself, are you? Want some dinner?'

He responded with another meow then padded into the kitchen. She wondered if he was actually hungry because she was well aware that he frequented the homes of several elderly ladies in the village who probably allowed him access to their cheese. Willy had a thing about cheese and would do just about anything to get it, as Lila knew from past experience. She didn't mind him paying visits to other people because he always came home to see her and Ethan, but she did worry about the impact of too much dairy on his weight and heart health. He was a funny little cat, an important member of her family, and she hoped he would be okay when the baby came along.

There was so much to think about …

4

LILA

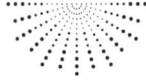

'What do you think?' Ethan asked as he stood back to survey the wall of the nursery.

'It's perfect.' Lila slid her arm through his and gazed at the mural he'd painted. He wasn't just good at things like carpentry and painting, he was also quite artistic. On the dark blue wall where the cot would go, Ethan had painted a mural of a woodland scene including all sorts of animals, plants and trees. It had taken him some time to get it right but now it was finished, it looked incredible. He'd got up very early to put the finishing touches to it, only waking Lila when it was done to get her opinion. 'In fact, I just want to lie down and gaze at it all day.'

Ethan kissed the top of her head. 'I'm glad you like it but I'm afraid that's out of the question.'

'I know.' Lila pouted. 'I have to go and try to find a dress.'

'You don't want to?' His eyes were filled with concern.

'It's not that I don't want to go shopping for a wedding dress, because I do, but I'm worried I won't find anything that fits. I also have no idea what type of dress I want.'

He smiled. 'Lila, you could buy a sack if you wanted and I know you'd still look incredible, but I'm sure you'll find something to wear. You're not as big as you think you are at all.'

Lila looked down at herself. 'Ethan, I've surrendered to the necessity for maternity clothes now because I got to the point where I couldn't even pull my leggings up over my thighs.'

'You're pregnant and your shape is changing. It doesn't mean it's a bad shape, just a different one.'

'I know, and I'm happy to be pregnant, I truly am, but it's taking time to get used to getting rounder. I look like I've swallowed a spacehopper.'

He laughed. 'A very small spacehopper and for what it's worth, I think you're sexier than ever.'

He pulled her into his arms and tilted her chin then held her gaze. His eyes were filled with love and happiness and she could see that the changes in his life had brought him joy. Before they got together, the loss of his wife, Tilly, had broken him but Lila had been able to watch over him as he healed. Since she found out she was pregnant, Ethan had seemed even happier and she knew he was looking forward to becoming a husband and father.

'You do, don't you?'

'I do.' He kissed her and delicious tingles ran over her skin. 'What time are you leaving?'

'In about an hour.'

'Well let's see if those maternity jeans need adjusting, shall we?'

'Ethan!' Lila giggled as he gently scooped her up and carried her out of the nursery and across the landing to their bedroom.

~

'OH MY GOD this is so good!' Joanne moaned as she took another bite of cake, her eyes closed, holding her fork so it was hovering in the air above her plate.

Roxie winked at Lila. 'Joanne, you're meant to eat it, not make love to it.'

Joanne opened her eyes. 'Try it and see how incredible it is.'

They'd come to the large shopping centre to look for a wedding dress for Lila and Roxie and Joanne were going to see if they could find outfits too. The centre was only thirty-five minutes away from Wisteria Hollow but when they got there Joanne had insisted that they visit a coffee shop first because she said her blood sugar was low and she also needed the loo.

Roxie held up a hand. 'No thanks, honey. I'm full of coffee after the three we've just had.'

'Lucky you.' Lila pulled a face. 'Herbal tea's fine but I do miss a good coffee.'

'You can have one, can't you?' Roxie asked. 'One won't hurt, surely?'

'I could but I'm trying to be sensible.' Lila sipped her peppermint tea. 'It's all for a good cause.'

'Indeed it is.' Roxie nodded. 'Right, Joanne, are you done?'

Joanne scraped her fork across the plate then licked it clean and smiled at them.

'I am done. And boy am I glad I had the chocolate fudge cake.'

'Let's go then shall we?'

Lila pushed her chair back slowly then hooked her bag over her shoulder. 'I guess so.'

'Come on, Lila, it'll be fine. You'll find something nice to wear.'

Lila hoped Roxie was right because she didn't feel that optimistic. Even though her day had gone well so far with a lovely start with Ethan then a good natter with Roxie and Joanne, the thought of trying on clothes did not appeal. She wasn't that keen on clothes shopping even when she wasn't pregnant, so now that she was, the prospect of trying things on was even more daunting. She also had some reservations, she knew, because of last time and didn't want to bring all those memories back.

'Trust your Aunty Roxie. All will be well.'

Lila forced a smile as Roxie took her hand and led her out of the coffee shop and into the bright shopping centre where most of the roof was made of glass and sunlight bounced off every surface. She winced at the brightness as her eyes adjusted, then gazed around her in awe. There were three floors to the shopping centre and on each one, colourful shopfronts displayed all sorts of wares including electrical goods, jewellery, toys, clothes and shoes. If she'd come here alone, she wouldn't have had a clue where to start, but Roxie and Joanne were expert shoppers and so she'd let them be her guides.

'Let's start with that one.' Roxie pointed at what was clearly a bridal shop.

'Oh … but I don't want a traditional dress, Rox. We agreed no bridal shops, remember?'

'Of course I do, sweetie, but I was thinking that they'll have more than white gowns in there and they might even have something suitable for me or Joanne.'

Lila paused, uncertain that this was the right move.

'If we don't look, we'll never know.'

'Can we go in that one next then?' Lila pointed at what appeared to be a bohemian clothing store with patchwork dungarees, coloured lace-up boots and floppy hats on the mannequins in the window.

'If you like, Lila, but you're not wearing dungarees to your wedding. I have to toe the line at that.'

Lila laughed. 'I wasn't thinking about them for the wedding, but they do look incredibly comfortable and would be nice to see me through the rest of this pregnancy.'

She cradled her bump and Roxie and Joanne looked down at it too.

'All right then, but bridalwear first.'

'Deal.' Lila nodded and off they went.

5

ROXIE

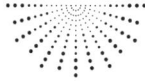

*T*he bridal shop was sparkly. It was the only word that came to mind as they walked inside. On every surface, on every visible garment, everything sparkled with rhinestones and sequins. On the shelves, tiaras and jewelled hair clips sparkled, while on displays set up around the shop, embellished shoes and sandals sparkled.

'Wow.' Joanne gawked at the array of gowns, tiaras, shoes and sandals. 'It's like someone sneezed glitter over everything.'

Lila reached out and placed a hand on Roxie's shoulder. 'Rox … it's so bright.'

'I know. However, I do think we should have a look around. There might just be something … slightly … understated here.'

'I doubt it.' Joanne was shaking her head. 'There are some seriously fancy outfits in here and look at the wigs. RuPaul would be completely at home in this place. It's enough to give you a migraine.'

Lila giggled. 'Wigs. Whatever for?'

Roxie gave a shrug. 'Some people like big hair on their wedding day.'

'What a great idea.' Joanne's eyes widened. 'You could have the wig styled, then on the morning of your wedding all you'd need to do is just pop it on and hey presto, you're ready!'

Lila ran a hand over her hair. 'It's something to consider, I guess. I could even go for a different colour.'

'I can just see Ethan being happy about that if you turn up at the vineyard with blue hair or black or … scarlet.' Roxie snorted.

'It would certainly make him look twice.'

The three of them laughed as they walked deeper into the shop and started to browse the rails.

'They've got plenty of different styles anyway,' Joanne said as she held up an ivory strapless number with a sequin bodice. She held it against her and swayed from side to side. 'What do you think?'

'It would look gorgeous on you but it's not for me.' Lila shook her head. 'Not this time.'

Joanne nodded and hung the dress back on the rail.

'Good morning.' A short woman with a glossy chestnut bob and round glasses appeared from behind the rail. Roxie jumped and she saw Lila and Joanne stiffen.

'Where did you come from?' Joanne asked, tactless as ever.

The woman gave a loud chuckle. 'I'm sorry if I startled you. The problem with being four foot eight is that people often miss me as they come in, especially if I'm behind one of the rails. I was just over there stacking some packets of stockings on the display. Anyway, my name's Barbara and this is my boutique. Barbara's Boutique.' She flashed them a warm smile. 'What can I help you with?'

'My friend here's getting married.' Roxie gestured at Lila.

'How wonderful.' Barbara clapped her hands together. Then her eyes landed on Lila's belly. 'Oh …'

Lila's hands flew to her bump protectively.

'How far along are you, dearie?' Barbara's eyes were glued to Lila's middle.

'Six months.'

'I see … So what kind of dress were you thinking of?'

Lila nibbled at her bottom lip. 'I'm not sure.'

'Not sure?' Barbara pursed her lips. 'You'll be limited from wearing some styles unless we alter them, but that shouldn't be a problem. I have a wonderful seamstress who does all the alterations very quickly. We'd probably have to go for a larger size then get it taken in around the shoulders.' She pulled a tape measure from around her neck and held it out. 'Let's have a look at you, shall we?'

Lila was silent and seemed, Roxie thought, quite terrified. Roxie put up a hand.

'I think we'd like to have a look around first,' she said. 'Get an idea of what you have available.'

'Of course.' Barbara inclined her head. 'But bear in mind that anything with a heavily beaded bodice will be difficult to alter. It will cost more too.'

'We'll bear that in mind.' Roxie took Lila's hand and led her towards the back of the store where there was a sale rack. 'You okay?'

'Yes. I just saw the dresses and it took me back to last time and then Barbara came at me with the tape measure and I froze.'

'Well we can't have that.' Roxie's protective instinct had kicked in and she wanted to whisk her friends out of the shop immediately. 'In your condition you need to avoid stress.'

'I'm all right.' Lila nodded. 'It was just a bit strange more than anything. I didn't want to offend Barbara and yet I didn't want to be measured right now. I get enough of that at maternity appointments when the midwife measures my belly.'

'And that's fine, honey. You don't have to do anything you don't want to do.'

'Shall we go?' Joanne cocked an eyebrow. 'No point staying in here if Lila feels rubbish about it.'

'Yes, let's leave.'

But Lila had gone quiet. She stepped forwards and lifted a dress from the sale rack. 'Look at this.'

'It's beautiful.' Roxie touched the material.

It was a Jane Austen style dress, in champagne silk, gathered in below the bust with capped sleeves and a round neckline.

'You'd look wonderful in that.' Joanne took the hanger from her and held it against Lila and the three of them nodded.

'Do you want to try the dress on?' Barbara had appeared at Lila's side. 'It might just fit.'

'Yes please.'

'The changing room is this way.' Barbara led them past the counter and to an open cubicle. 'Just pull the curtain across then call me when you're ready and I can help with the buttons up the back.'

'Thanks.'

Lila closed the curtain behind her and Roxie and Joanne waited.

'I have another customer, so I'll go and serve her then come back.' Barbara shuffled away.

Roxie and Joanne waited.

And waited.

And waited some more.

The customer Barbara was serving left and others came in.

'How long's she been in there?' Joanne whispered.

'I'm not sure but I'm going to check if she needs help. Hold this for me.' Roxie gave Joanne her handbag and went to the curtain. 'Knock! Knock!'

'Who is it?'

'Roxie of course.'

'Come in quick.' Lila's voice was muffled as if she was speaking through a mask.

Roxie slipped past the curtain and gasped. 'Goodness, Lila, what happened?'

'I don't know. I thought I had to put it on over my head and then I couldn't get it down over my belly, so I tried to pull it off and now I'm stuck.'

'Why didn't you call me?'

'I was too embarrassed.'

Lila was in the middle of the changing room with the dress covering her top half like some kind of giant sweet wrapper and her arms sticking out the top, while her bottom half was exposed revealing a large pair of yellow maternity knickers and white ankle socks that Roxie suspected might belong to Ethan.

'Okay, I'm going to try and undo the mess you've created. Hold still.'

Lila's hands were held in place above her head and Roxie could see why she was trapped. Roxie ran her hands over the bunched-up material, trying to find an opening. When she did, she fiddled about with it until she found some buttons.

'Lila, you didn't undo all the buttons before you tried to pull it on.' Roxie slid them from the holes and soon had some give in the material. She wriggled it from side to side and soon pulled it from Lila's head and arms. 'There you go!'

Lila staggered as she was freed and blew out a long breath. 'Thank you!'

Roxie shook her head. Lila's face was bright red, her hair was sticking up like she'd been dragged through a hedge and her swollen belly made her look like she'd swallowed a football.

'Do you want me to help you put it on properly?' Roxie straightened the dress and shook it out but Lila shook her head.

'If it's a tight fit now it'll be no good in four weeks.'

'Such a shame as it's so pretty.'

'It's gorgeous but I think I was pushing my luck.'

'Fear not, we'll find something for you.'

Roxie hung the dress back on the hanger then ducked out of the changing room while Lila got dressed again.

'Any luck?' Joanne asked.

'It's not quite right.' Roxie smiled sadly as Joanne passed her handbag back.

'That's a shame but we'll find something.' Joanne patted Roxie's back. 'But perhaps we need to grab some refreshments first.'

'Joanne, really? We haven't long had coffee.'

'I know but Lila probably needs a cold drink now.'

'All right then.' Joanne was probably right as Lila had looked flustered when she'd been freed from the dress. 'Refreshments it is.'

When Lila emerged from the changing room, they thanked Barbara then left the shop in search of another café. There must be a dress out there for Lila surely, something that would make her feel beautiful on her special day and something that would be very different from the one she'd bought last time.

Roxie was determined to help Lila to find that dress.

6
LILA

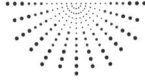

A full day of shopping had led to purchases being made but the main one, the wedding dress, had not been found. After the humiliation of getting stuck in the champagne Jane Austen dress and being forced to have Roxie help her get free while she stood there in her big yellow undies and white socks – that actually belonged to Ethan and had been all Lila could find that morning – Lila hadn't wanted to try anything else on.

Instead, she'd encouraged Roxie and Joanne to find outfits for the wedding, which they had, and Lila had been content to purchase a pair of gold sandals with a small heel that would go with most outfits and a new pearly pink lipstick that Joanne said would be perfect for a wedding. They'd had several stops for refreshments through the course of the day because Joanne had insisted she needed to eat and drink regularly. Lila suspected, however, that Joanne was also looking out for her and believed that with Lila being pregnant, she needed plenty of breaks from walking around.

It had been a very pleasant day but when Lila had arrived home, she'd been unable to escape the sense of disappointment at not finding something to wear. Roxie had done her best to help her look but Lila just hadn't seen the right dress and now wondered if she would or if she'd be forced to wear jeans and a shirt to her own wedding.

Ethan had sent her a text to say he'd be working late as he wanted to get another coat on the large kitchen-diner of the renovation and so Lila had a few hours to spare. She had a soak in a bubble bath then put on her soft pyjamas and padded downstairs to the kitchen and made a mint tea. After she'd fed the cats, she took her tea through to the lounge, sank onto the sofa and turned on the TV.

The first thing to come on was a bridal programme about women whose fiancés were given a budget to plan their weddings. The grooms chose everything from bridal gown to flowers, venue to food, and it caused chaos with some of the brides who hated what had been chosen for them. Lila watched it, her thoughts repeatedly drawn to Ethan. Would he know what to choose for her? He'd thought the vineyard would be a good venue, and it was wonderful, so she thought he could probably get the dress and flowers right too. And, of course, Lila was no bridezilla so liked to think she wouldn't be that hard to please. The dress was only a source of consternation for her because she feared having something similar to last time and because she was pregnant and wanted to feel that she looked good on her wedding day for Ethan and for herself. She aimed to only have the one wedding, wanted to spend her life with Ethan, and so it would be nice to have a day they could treasure and photographs that they could show to their children and one day, perhaps even their grandchildren.

A fluttering in her tummy made her press her hand to her bump and she was rewarded with a kick. She'd been feeling the baby move for weeks now but with each day the feelings grew stronger as the baby grew bigger. Sometimes she felt sure that the baby reacted to her voice and to Ethan's, and a few times even to the cats when they meowed.

She was so lucky to have this baby, so lucky to have a man as good as Ethan to love her; she had so much that many others didn't. The fact that she'd had such a lonely childhood with cold and disinterested parents and then been jilted at the altar by the first man she'd allowed herself to love made her very aware of how her life had changed. She had a loving fiancé, a baby on the way, two adorable cats, a warm cosy home, a kind and caring mother-in-law to be, wonderful friends and she lived in a beautiful friendly village. Life was good for Lila now and she'd never take it for granted.

And yet … there was something missing. It wasn't her parents because how could she miss something she'd never had? There was something else, someone else, she'd never told anyone about since she'd walked away and cut her parents from her life. When she had finally accepted that they would never be the people she wanted them to be, let it sink in that they had no interest in her whatsoever and never would do, she'd felt free. But the hardest thing to do had been leaving the other person behind, and Lila's way of coping had been not allowing thoughts of that person, not even so much as a name, to enter her mind.

But now Lila was carrying a child and as the pregnancy progressed, she had found it harder and harder not to think of that person, of how they had grown up together and known each other inside out. Or so she'd thought until there had been a decision to make and Lila had not been chosen.

She took some slow deep breaths and tried to push the pain away. It was grief that she was feeling, something she'd felt initially but that had faded as the years had passed and she'd trained herself not to think about it. If she didn't let it enter her mind, then how could it hurt her? She'd been good at pushing it away, expert in fact, and even Ben hadn't known that Lila had lost more than her parents because Lila had never told anyone; not her friends, not Ben and not Ethan. That made her feel bad because they'd shared so much but how could she tell him now? Ethan knew that her parents couldn't care less about her so how could she add to that with news of another person who should love her but didn't? It could change how he saw her, change how anyone saw her because what kind of person had close family members that hated them?

There was a tickle on her cheek and she raised her hand to find that it was wet. She shook her head. Here she was indulging in self-pity that was surely no good for her and in turn no good for the baby. She had to put these sad thoughts from her mind and move on just like everyone else had done.

A knock at the door snapped her from her thoughts and she went to answer it.

'Oh … hello Freda.' Lila smiled at Ethan's mother. 'Everything okay?'

Freda nodded her grey head. 'I'm fine, sweetie. Better than you by the looks of it.'

Lila pushed her hair behind her ears. 'I'm okay. Don't I look it?'

'You look exhausted.'

'Oh … Well, I was out all day shopping with Roxie and Joanne and those two can shop until they drop, so I guess I am a bit tired.'

'You look like you've been crying, Lila.' Freda's eyes were so filled with concern that Lila felt the sadness bubbling inside her again and her vision blurred. 'Can I come in?'

'Of course. Sorry … I didn't … mean … to keep you … on the doorstep.' Lila's tears were falling freely now as the disappointment at the lack of success with dress shopping and her thoughts about her family swirled around inside her.

'Don't worry about that.' Freda ushered Lila inside and closed the door then set down a large bag she'd brought with her. 'Do you want me to call Ethan?'

'No … it's okay. I'll be fine. I … think … it's hormones.'

'Yes, of course it is. I was like that when I was pregnant with Ethan. Sobbed for nine months, I did, without a break.' Freda patted Lila's back. 'Come on, let me make you a cup of tea and explain why I'm here.'

'You don't have to explain why you're visiting.'

'No, I know that, but I'm also not going to be an overpowering mother-in-law who turns up and takes over. I'll be here if you, Ethan or the baby need me, but I'll never be a nuisance. I'd hate to be one of *those* women.'

'You could never be like that, Freda, you're far too nice.'

They went through to the kitchen and Lila filled the kettle and switched it on. When they had mugs of decaffeinated tea, they went to the lounge and sat down on the sofa.

'Right then, Lila. I happened to see Roxie earlier. She was out with Fletcher, walking the dogs, and I asked if you'd found a dress. She told me that there was nothing you liked at all and it got me thinking. You're a very creative person and excellent with knitting needles, crochet and a sewing machine, so if you can't find the dress you want in a shop, why not make it?'

Lila sat back and sipped her tea.

'Make it?'

'Of course. I've seen the greyhounds and other soft toys you've crocheted, the baby clothes and blankets you've made, the beautiful patchwork coverlets and cushion covers. Haven't you ever made a dress?'

'Not for some time.'

'But you could do it.'

'Probably. Yes … I think I could.'

'So … I had a dig around in my loft because I knew I had some patterns there as well as some material. I used to make a lot of things years ago and have some fabulous patterns from the seventies and eighties, and some material that I bought a few years back and never used. You could make something a bit retro or adapt the patterns to suit what it is that you want.'

'That's a really good idea, Freda.'

'Thank you. I'm quite pleased with myself if I'm honest. Roxie didn't say too much but I could tell that she was worried about you. She did confess that she felt disappointed with herself for not finding something you liked but I told her I'd see what I could do.'

'I'm so grateful.'

'Well … let's look at the patterns and material first, before you thank me, just in case you don't like what I've brought. The material might not be right, but it doesn't matter because we can go and pick something else up tomorrow and take it from there.'

Lila sniffed, worried she was about to start crying again. 'You're really kind.'

'And so are you. Lila, I'm so glad that Ethan found you. After he lost Tilly, I was worried he'd spend the rest of his life alone. I mean … he adored her and he was bereft after she died but then he came home to the village and met you and I couldn't wish for a lovelier wife for him. You two are perfect for each other and now you have a baby on the way and my heart is filled with joy. I can't even explain how happy I am.' She pressed a hand to her chest and blinked hard.

'Stop it or you'll set us both off.' Lila laughed. 'It doesn't take much for me at the moment.'

Freda started to laugh too and Cleo and Willy looked up at them from the rug in front of the fireplace as if confused about why the humans were behaving so weirdly.

'Right, I'm going to get my bag from the hallway and we can have a look at what I've brought and start planning.'

'Wonderful.'

Lila hugged herself and smiled because even though her life had been difficult in some ways in the past, it was certainly making up for it now.

7

JOANNE

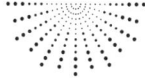

'What do you think of this one?' Joanne turned her laptop around so Max could see the screen. 'It has a shower room downstairs, two bedrooms upstairs and a lounge along with a … somewhat cosy kitchen.'

He peered at the screen and she saw his brow concertina.

'You don't like it?'

'Not really. The kitchen is more cramped than cosy.' He met her gaze. 'Do you like it?'

'Not really. If we're aiming to buy our forever home, I don't think that's it.'

He sipped his coffee then his cheeks flushed as he asked, 'Do you think two bedrooms will be enough anyway?'

Something fluttered inside Joanne. 'Why?'

'Well … you know.'

'No, I don't.' Joanne looked around the café, but it was quiet now. It was ten-fifteen and the breakfast rush had been and gone and Max had come to spend her break with her. 'Tell me what it is that I'm supposed to know.'

'Well …' He pushed his glasses up his nose and blinked at her. 'What if … a few years down the road … we decided that we wanted to add to our family?'

'I don't get you.' She frowned but the side of her mouth twitched. She loved teasing him.

'What I mean is–'

'If we got a dog?'

'No.' He shook his head. 'Not that I don't want a dog, or a cat, but that wasn't quite was I was getting at. You don't give a dog its own bedroom, do you?'

Joanne smiled. 'You could do.'

'You could do, yes, but don't they usually sleep downstairs.'

'I guess some do.'

'Anyway …' He licked his lips. 'What if we decide we might like to have … uh … children?'

'Children!' She fanned her face with her hands. 'My goodness, Max, you have taken me by surprise.'

'Really?' His cheeks were bright red now and he'd started rubbing the back of his neck.

'No.' She shook her head and took his hand. 'Of course it's something I'd like to think we might consider in time. I love you, Max, and the idea of having children with you is wonderful. I'd never felt the urge to procreate before and was convinced that being aunt to my niece and nephew was sufficient, but since we got together … something's started to change.'

'You made me work for that one, didn't you?' His blush was fading slowly and Joanne felt a rush of love for him.

'I did and I know I shouldn't tease you but you're just adorable when you get flustered.'

'Thanks.'

'Hey … I love you.'

'I love you more.' He raised her hand and kissed it.

Before Christmas, they had talked about buying a place in the new year or even staying on at Max's so they could save their money and go on some luxury holidays, but something had kept them scouring the property sites. Joanne knew that it was part curiosity and part desire to find exactly the right home to settle in and it seemed that the process would continue until they found that home.

'Oi, you two, get a room.' It was Joanne's boss, Bridget Wibberley. 'Can't have you putting our customers off their teacakes, can we?' She grinned at them exposing her large teeth complete with a tiny diamond that she'd had glued to her left incisor.

'Sorry, Bridget.' Joanne nodded at her.

'I'm pulling your leg, Joanne.' Bridget picked up their mugs off the table. 'Want another coffee?'

'That would be lovely, thanks.'

'What're you looking at anyway? From over there it looked like you were planning world domination with your heads together as you gazed at the computer screen.'

'Not quite world domination, more like trying to get a grip of the local property market,' Joanne said.

'I thought you had a place?'

'We do.' Joanne nodded. 'But Max bought it before we got together and while it's nice—'

'We'd like something a bit bigger and something that we've chosen together,' Max explained. 'We're, uh, thinking we want somewhere to be our forever home.'

'Bigger, eh?' Bridget toyed with the pencil that was tucked behind her ear. 'Listen … you know I lost my mum and inherited her place?'

'Yes.' Joanne watched her boss's face carefully.

'Well, I'm having her cottage renovated. Ethan Morris is doing a wonderful job and it's going to be absolutely gorgeous when it's finished. Anyway, you could have a look at that if you like. No pressure if it's not right for you and you'd have to bear in mind that the work isn't finished yet, but it looks good already and it could be what you're looking for. There are four bedrooms, two bathrooms, a large kitchen-diner, two reception rooms, off road parking …' She shrugged. 'Have a think and if you'd like to take a look, you're very welcome. You know where it is, don't you, Joanne?'

'I do.'

'Something to think about anyway. No one's seen it yet because I'm not planning on putting it up for sale until the work is done.'

'Thanks.'

'I'll get your coffees.'

Bridget headed back to the counter and Max raised his eyebrows. 'Sounds amazing.'

'It's a lovely cottage and I know Ethan will do a wonderful job but I have a feeling it might be out of our price range.'

'You never know.'

'Well, we have my savings, thanks to my parents.'

'And we have the equity in the place we already have.'

Joanne smiled. She loved that he spoke about the cottage as if it was theirs even though he'd bought it before they got together. He was serious about sharing things, about making a life together as partners and it was one of the things that Joanne loved about him.

'Plus …' He flashed her a grin. 'I have a little put aside too.'

'You do?'

He tapped the side of his nose. 'Saving for a rainy day, so to speak. I was going to use it to take you on a gorgeous holiday as we discussed or to pay for our, ahem, wedding … but we could put it towards a deposit on a house.'

'Our wedding?' Joanne missed the end of his sentence because he'd used the 'W' word.

'Well, you know, it's one of the things I thought we could discuss this year.'

'That is a lot of information to process in one morning, Max.'

'I know, but sometimes I think it's better just to go for it when the time is right.'

'Getting married or sharing your thoughts?'

'All of the above.' He laughed. 'Why not, Joanne? You only live once and I'm madly in love with you so yes, let's get a bigger place, get married and have babies.'

Joanne had to force her mouth closed. Max was sweet and kind, gorgeous and goofy. He loved reading and writing and cooking and spending time with her in a way no man ever had done before. He adored her curves and her wavy hair and accepted her exactly as she was, with her appetite for cake and chocolate, her frequent loud farts (that she'd long since given up trying to hold in) and all. She never felt judged by him and it was refreshing because she knew she was sometimes a bit much for some people, but Max never seemed fazed by her at all.

Max was, indeed, her perfect man.

Bridget returned with their coffees and set them down on the table.

'Bridget?'

'Yes?' The older woman nodded, making her large silver earrings wobble.

'We'd like to have a look at the cottage if that's okay?'

'Of course it is. Let me know when's good for you. If I'm working, I'm sure Ethan can let you in and show you around.'

'Wonderful.'

Joanne sucked in a deep breath and wriggled on her chair and Max took her hand. 'You're excited now aren't you?'

'Incredibly excited.'

'Your effervescence is one of the things that makes you amazing. Life will never be dull with you around.'

As he leant towards her and kissed her, Joanne felt like all her dreams had come true at once.

8

LILA

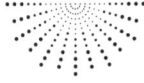

'*I* love this, Lila,' Roxie said as Lila spread the silk out across her dining table.

'It's beautiful, isn't it?'

'And the chiffon too. Freda gave this to you?'

'She did and the pattern I've chosen.'

'Can I see it?'

Lila nodded and went to the kitchen dresser, opened a drawer and retrieved the pattern. 'I've kept it hidden because I don't want Ethan to see it before our wedding day.'

'Wow! I love it and in those materials, it will be simple yet stunning.'

'I was thinking though …'

'Yes?'

'Should I get one of those wigs to go with it?'

'What?' Roxie's eyes widened.

'Well they did have some fabulous ones and a blue one would be just …' Lila started laughing. 'Sorry, I can't do it! Your face …' She held her belly as she laughed. 'I'm joking.'

'Thank goodness for that. Blue hair has its place but not on your wedding day. If you usually had blue, green or pink hair, then fair enough but you have the loveliest blonde locks and you should show them off.'

'Thank you.'

'What about a veil or tiara or something?'

Lila shook her head. 'I've had an idea about that and I think you can help me.'

'Ooh, okay. I'm excited to know more.'

'Let's get the kettle on and have some of those cookies you baked and I'll show you the designs I've drawn.'

'Wonderful.'

Half an hour later, they were sitting in the lounge. The windows were open and warm rose scented air floated into the room along with the sounds of a lawnmower in a neighbouring garden and the birds singing in the trees that lined Sunflower Street.

'I think your idea is fabulous,' Roxie said as she relaxed on the sofa, her bare feet propped up on the coffee table, her turquoise toenails matching her soft silk blouse.

'I'm glad. It just seemed perfect to go with the dress and sandals.'

'It will be. Oh, Lila, Ethan will be wowed by you when you walk down that aisle.'

'I hope so.'

'Of course he will and I'm going to be so proud.' She sniffed and pulled a tissue from the box on the table. 'I don't know how I'm going to do it without crying all the way.'

'Don't or you'll start me off.'

'On the subject of weddings … what are we doing for your hen night?'

'Ugh … I was hoping to avoid one of those.' Lila had never been keen on the whole hen and stag thing and didn't want any fuss anyway.

'Noooo. You can't say that. It's part of the fun.'

You know me, Rox, I'm not a big party animal and I can't drink at the moment anyway.'

'It doesn't have to be a boozy night. We could have afternoon tea or something nice and civilised. I know … we could have a garden party at mine. Have tea and cakes in the garden and some champagne for those who want it and just celebrate the life you've had and the one you're embarking upon.'

'It's not going to be that different.' Lila cradled her mug between her hands.

'I guess not as you're already living together but you'll soon have a baby and things will change a lot then.'

'That's true.'

'And being married isn't a massive change but it can kind of cement things. To be honest, Lila, I just want to have a party for you before you get married so we can celebrate love and friendship and good fortune. Life can be so difficult and I think it's very important to make the most of the good times.'

'You're right. Let's do it.'

'Thank you!' Roxie smiled. 'I'll make it wonderful, I promise.'

'We could go strawberry picking beforehand to make sure we've got some lovely fruit.'

'That's a wonderful idea. I love strawberry picking.'

'Me too. And now I'm craving big, fat, red strawberries with clotted cream. That would be so yummy right now.'

'With meringues and scones and pink champagne.'

'All of that except for the champagne.'

They laughed together.

'What can we have instead?' Roxie asked. 'I'm rather peckish now.'

'We've just eaten the cookies you made.'

'I know but I fancy something fruity.'

'There's ice cream in the freezer. It's some raspberry swirl thing that Ethan picked up at the weekend.'

'That sounds perfect. Shall I get us a bowl each?'

'Go on then but I think I'll have to plan on making the size up in the wedding dress if you keep feeding me like this.'

'You're perfect the way you are and don't you forget it. Right, two bowls of raspberry swirl thingy coming right up!'

Roxie took their mugs to the kitchen and Lila stroked her bump. 'I hope you're okay in there, little one. There's a lot going on right now.' The baby gave a kick that Lila felt against her palm. 'I'll take that as a yes.'

9
ROXIE

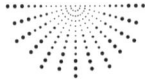

*H*eading home after spending the morning with Lila, Roxie's mind was busy. There was a lot to organise, but she liked being busy and was so happy for her friends. When the people she cared about were happy and settled, Roxie could relax and enjoy life. Her thoughts turned to Fletcher, Glenda and Stinky. She'd only been away a few hours but she was looking forward to getting home and seeing them all again. Having her own little family was the best feeling in the world. She was glad that Fletcher had thought to adopt Stinky because Glenda adored her and was enjoying having a canine companion far more than Roxie could ever have imagined. It made her wonder why they hadn't got another dog years ago, but then she realised that if they had, she wouldn't have been able to enjoy those years alone with Glenda.

Her mobile buzzed in her bag so she got it out and swiped the screen. It was Fletcher asking her to pick up some bread and some chocolate chips. He was baking cookies because the ones Roxie had made that morning had, rather strangely he claimed, disappeared. Roxie laughed then sent a reply and changed direction to head to the shop. She'd have a look and pick something up for the dogs too because she didn't like to return empty-handed.

Ten minutes later, Roxie emerged from the grocery shop with a paper bag containing chocolate chips, crusty bread and a tin of sardines. Much as she wasn't keen on the smell of sardines, the dogs loved them and the oil was good for their skin. She knew that as soon as Glenda saw the tin she'd go crazy as she always did and race around the house while Roxie opened the sardines and spooned them into the dogs' bowls. Stinky would, of course, copy her older sister, and Roxie and Fletcher would end up laughing indulgently.

She lowered her sunglasses from her hair and rested the bag on her hip then set off for home. As she walked, she greeted a few people, waved at Joanne as she passed the café and breathed in the balmy air. It was a beautiful day and …

'Lila?' She frowned because her friend was standing outside the library gate reading the noticeboard. When she'd left Lila, she'd said something about taking a nap, but now she was out and about already and wearing different clothes. Roxie looked both ways then crossed the road, waving to get Lila's attention. Lila glanced at her, folded her paper and marched away.

Roxie lowered her glasses to get a better look at the retreating woman.

It had certainly looked like Lila. The face shape, hair colour and petite figure were the same and yet there was something off.

That was it! The woman Roxie had seen didn't have a baby bump. She was, in fact, very slim and Roxie had caught a glimpse of a flat stomach under a tight white T-shirt. Roxie shrugged and turned for home. There were often tourists in Wisteria Hollow in the summer months and it just so happened that the woman she'd just seen looked a bit like Lila. Didn't they say everyone had a double out there somewhere?

10

JOANNE

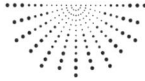

'Hello!' Joanne called as she pushed the front door of the cottage open. 'Anyone here? It's Joanne and Max.'

She turned to Max and he shrugged so they entered the cool dark hallway.

'Ethan?'

She heard footsteps from above their heads and then Ethan was on the landing. 'Hey there.' He padded down the stairs to greet them.

'Hey mate.' Max shook Ethan's hand. 'How's it going?'

'We're getting there. The plumber's in the bathroom fitting new pipes so he can put the bathroom in, then he's going to do the kitchen.'

'It really is a full renovation then?' Joanne asked as she peered around.

'Everything has been ripped out, except for irreplaceable features like beams and the slate floor in the kitchen and the whole cottage is being rewired. It will have all the original charm but with energy efficiency and speedy Wi-Fi.' Ethan's cheeks were flushed and there were tiny beads of perspiration at his hairline from manual labour and the warmth of the day. 'You want the grand tour?'

'If you have time?' Joanne smiled.

'Of course, I have. I could do with a break anyway. Cutting in is challenging and can't be rushed. Let's do the downstairs first.'

Ethan led them around the ground floor, showing them the two large reception rooms, the small snug that could be a study or, as Max suggested, a games room then he took them through to the kitchen-diner. It was a large open space and he showed them where the kitchen units would be, the island and then the room for a dresser and table and chairs. Bifold doors opened out onto an established garden and when they stepped outside, Joanne felt breathless at the beauty before her. When Max took her hand and squeezed it, she knew he felt the same.

'This is some garden,' Joanne said.

'It's pretty cool, right?' Ethan agreed. 'The old lady who lived here liked her flower beds and trees and there's more past the first section.'

'You mean it's bigger than it looks?'

He nodded. 'See the archway in the hedge?'

Joanne peered at what she'd thought was the end of the garden, thinking the archway led to a gate or even a garage.

'If you go through there, you'll find a whole fruit and vegetable garden.'

'Can we have a look now?'

'Sure, carry on.' Ethan nodded. 'I'll be inside if you need me and can show you round upstairs when you're ready.'

'Thank you.' Max smiled.

'Let's explore, shall we?'

Joanne led him over the grass and towards the hedge. They went through the narrow opening and it was like entering the set of a gardening show. There were rows of fruit trees, raised beds with herbs and vegetables and a small greenhouse where what looked like tomato plants were reaching for the sky.

'Max, it's so beautiful. Can you imagine living here?'

Max was gazing around them, his eyes wide behind his glasses. 'The house is worth it for the garden alone.'

'We could live on the produce from the garden.' Joanne wasn't sure why, but her throat was aching with emotion.

Max pulled her against his chest and kissed her forehead. 'I love it. Do you?'

'I really do.'

'I think we should put in an offer.'

'But it's not finished yet.'

'I don't care. This is the home we're meant to have.'

'Max!' Joanne giggled. 'You're so romantic sometimes.'

He nodded. 'I blame all the reading I do. I must be absorbing a lot of things without realising it and being around you brings it to the surface.'

She looked into his eyes then slid her arms over his shoulders. 'I love you so bloody much.'

'I love you too.'

He kissed her softly then hugged her hard and Joanne knew that they had to make an offer on the cottage. She knew that someone could make a better offer than them and that they'd be disappointed, but if it was meant to be, it was meant to be.

'Come on then, let's see the upstairs.'

Max wiggled his eyebrows so Joanne tapped his arm.

'Behave yourself.'

'I thought you liked it when I'm a bit … naughty.'

'I do but not now, Max.'

'I'm teasing you, my love. Let's go and check out the bedrooms and bathroom then we can go straight to the café and speak to Bridget.'

'Seriously?'

'I've never been more serious in my life, Joanne. I want this home for us and for … anyone else who might come along.'

'What? Other people?' she joked.

'You know full well what I mean.'

Joanne grinned as they headed inside, her heart fit to burst with excitement and hope.

11

LILA

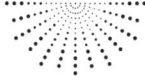

'*And* now exhale as you go down ...' Finlay Bridgewater touched the floor in front of him as easily as if he was made of rubber. 'Don't forget though, mums to be, don't push your bodies ... allow for your bumps.'

Lila stretched forwards gently but didn't try to achieve a full forwards fold pose because her belly wouldn't allow it. She breathed in and out, filling her lungs and focusing on nothing other than the feelings in her limbs and her breathing, knowing that this was good for her and good for the baby.

Roxie was to Lila's left, supple and bendy as Finlay, and Joanne was to her right. Lila was flanked by her besties, enjoying her Saturday morning yoga, feeling the peace that going through the poses and emptying her mind gave her.

A loud ripping noise from her right startled her and she wobbled as she tried to maintain her balance.

'Oops!' Joanne giggled.

'Joanne!' Roxie scolded as she reached for Lila. 'You okay, honey?'

'Yes, I'm fine thanks. I was completely relaxed but Joanne's fart broke my concentration, and I lost my balance.'

Joanne's face was red but Lila wasn't sure if it was embarrassment or the strain of trying to bend over.

'I'm so sorry. I just can't hold it in when I'm relaxing and that pose and downward dog get me every time.' Joanne shrugged. 'As long as you're okay, Lila?'

'I'm fine, I promise.' Lila nodded. She placed both hands over her bump, something she found herself doing automatically now in a protective maternal gesture. 'We're fine,' she said softly.

'Joanne, try avoiding eating beans and anything that gives you wind the night before yoga.' Roxie was frowning at Joanne. 'Honestly, I nearly went head first onto the floor too.'

Joanne looked down at her naked feet and Lila's heart went out to her. 'Hey, love, it's okay. It happens.'

'It most certainly does.' Finlay joined in from the stage. He was upright now, nodding his head at them. 'I don't think there's anyone who hasn't farted at some point when doing yoga.' He put his hands on his slim hips. 'Is there?' He looked around the hall.

There was a murmuring and shaking of heads.

'See, Joanne, everyone farts, some more than others, but we're just animals with digestive systems and yoga can relax those parts of us that other exercise can't reach.' He winked at Joanne and Lila saw her mouth 'Thank you.' Finlay waved a hand. 'Anyway, let's get you sweaty folks on your mats now to ease out any stiffness in your backs and shoulders.'

They all lay down and Lila felt how her body was supported by the mat, felt her limbs loosen and her heart rate slow again. She turned carefully onto her side and pulled the long narrow pregnancy pillow she'd brought with her under her bump and between her legs to support her body. The pillow was flexible, and she used it a lot now for yoga and in bed. She knew from antenatal appointments and from her reading that she had to be careful of lying on her back, as the baby and womb could put pressure on the blood vessels that supplied her uterus and affect the oxygen supply to the baby.

She listened to Finlay's relaxing voice as he led the class into deeper relaxation and let her mind focus on the baby in her womb, on what he or she looked like now and how her deep state of relaxation affected the tiny being too. The thought that she'd meet her child within months was at once wonderfully exciting and utterly terrifying but she knew it would all be okay. Lila and Ethan would be completely responsible for another person – physically, emotionally and mentally. It was an enormous responsibility and one that she vowed to take seriously. Her baby would want for nothing, would be loved, cared for and raised in a happy home.

'Lilaaaa …'

She opened her eyes and peered up at Roxie's smiling face.

'Hello, darling. You must have dropped off.'

Lila yawned then Roxie helped her to sit up.

'I think I did. Last thing I remember I was thinking about the baby.'

'Aww.' Roxie sighed. 'That's lovely.'

'How long was I out?'

'I'm not sure because I was drifting for a while too. Finlay's sessions are just the best. When his voice stopped, I came round then looked over at you and you were fast asleep.'

'What about Joanne?' Lila turned to look and snorted. 'Hungry, huh?'

Joanne nodded as she munched on a cereal bar.

'Actually, I could eat now.'

'What do you fancy?'

'Eggs. And buttery toast. Mmmm. And tea. Decaff, of course.'

'Let's head to the café, then.'

Roxie took Lila's hands and helped her up. They put their trainers on while Joanne finished her snack and rolled up her mat then she did the same with Lila's mat to save her from having to bend down again. Her friends were taking such good care of her.

'To the café!' Joanne held her mat up as if it was a spear then jogged out of the hall and Roxie and Lila followed, shouting their thanks to Finlay as they went.

≈

IN THE CAFÉ, Lila placed her bag, mat and long pillow on the wide windowsill then sat down and sighed. She'd enjoyed the session and been surprised by how quickly she'd dropped off to sleep, although yoga was so relaxing that she shouldn't be. It made her feel loose and refreshed afterwards, like she'd had a holiday and that had to be good for her and the baby.

Roxie returned from the toilet and sat down.

'Did Joanne order me a low-fat muffin, do you know?' Roxie asked as she sat down.

'I'm not sure. She's still talking to Bridget.' Lila gestured at the counter where Joanne and her boss were chatting away while Bridget multitasked.

When Joanne came and joined them, she set down three mugs on the table then frowned. 'No, that's not right. The pink mug is the decaff.' She moved the mugs around again then nodded. 'Bridget said the muffins are just out of the oven so will be about five minutes and Lila, your poached eggs on toast will be the same.'

'Lovely, thanks.' Lila glanced across at the counter where Bridget was bustling away, one of her employees at her side. The café was always busy and a successful little business.

'I did offer to help but she told me to go away.' Joanne giggled. 'Probably doesn't want me asking for overtime.'

'She thinks a lot of you, doesn't she?' Roxie asked.

'I know. I'm lucky to have such a fab boss.' Joanne raised her mug. 'To fab bosses everywhere.'

They clinked mugs, grinning at each other, because Roxie didn't work outside of the home and Lila was self-employed, so her friends were their own bosses.

'How did the viewing of Bridget's cottage go?' Lila asked Joanne. 'Ethan said he showed you round.'

'It's amazing.' Joanne's eyes widened. 'You should see the garden.'

'Good?' Roxie asked.

'Incredible. I've never seen anything like it. The inside of the cottage is a work in progress, but the garden is just perfect as it is. There are fruit trees and raised beds of vegetables and so many flowers in the borders. I could just sit out there for hours and watch the bees and butterflies visiting the garden while listening to the birdsong and enjoying the smell of honeysuckle, lavender and wisteria. My parents would prob-ably want to buy the cottage themselves if they saw it.'

'Have you spoken to Bridget yet?' Lila sipped her tea.

'Yes. We came straight here and waited for her to have her break then we made her an offer.'

'And?' Lila and Roxie asked together.

'She's considering it.' Joanne chewed at her bottom lip. 'We just really want it, but we're trying not to get our hopes up because we'll be devastated if someone else offers more. It's the first place we've seen that we really love. And … Max has started talking about how it would be the perfect home to raise children.'

'That's so exciting!' Lila clapped her hands. 'I hope you get it.'

'Me too. It's going to be amazing once the interior work is done. In reality, it's more than we considered paying but Max is convinced that we can manage it, so … We'll see.'

Bridget arrived with their food order and set it on the table. She smiled at them all and squeezed Joanne's shoulder. 'Can I get you anything else?'

'No this is wonderful, thanks.' Joanne smiled at her. 'Are you sure you don't need a hand?'

'It's your day off, Joanne, so have a bloody rest, won't you?' Bridget shook her head. 'Too generous for her own good, this one.'

'We think so.' Roxie nodded.

'Did she tell you she wants to buy my mum's old cottage?'

'She did.' Roxie's face had gone very still as if she didn't want to sway Bridget's decision.

'Well … I'm giving the offer very serious consideration.' Bridget winked. 'Very serious consideration indeed.'

Lila's stomach rolled as she imagined how Joanne must be feeling and she reached out and took her hand. Joanne met her gaze but Lila could see that she was uncertain.

'Oh Joanne, I'm pulling your leg.' Bridget puffed out her cheeks. 'Of course I'm going to accept your offer. I just had to speak to my solicitor about fees and all that horrible official stuff. I want you and Max to have the cottage and I know my dear old mum, God rest her soul, would want you to have it too. She'd hate for it to go to strangers and would love the thought of you two enjoying the garden and raising some babies there.'

Joanne pushed her chair back and stood up then threw herself at Bridget. 'Thank you! Thank you! Thank you!' When she pulled back, her hair was wild as it had fallen from its bun and stuck out like straw around her flushed cheeks. 'Oh my god! I need to tell Max.' She looked around her. 'I need to tell him now.'

'Go on then.' Lila laughed. 'We'll drop your things round for you if you don't make it back here.'

'Okay! Thank you. You're the best, Bridget. The absolute best!'

Joanne bolted for the door then froze, ran back and grabbed her muffin, then raced away again, waving at them through the window as she headed for the library.

'Well, that's settled then.' Bridget sniffed and wiped at her eyes before adjusting her apron. 'I've done my good deed for the day. Enjoy your breakfast ladies and shout if you want anything else.'

'Thanks.'

Lila smiled at Roxie, swallowing hard to stop herself from crying.

'Nothing like some good news on a Saturday, is there?' Roxie raised her muffin and took a bite.

'Definitely not,' Lila agreed.

'Oh …' Roxie put her muffin down and dusted her hands off on a serviette. 'I forgot to tell you that after I left your place the other day, I saw your double.'

'My double?'

'Yes. Outside the library I saw a woman who was your spitting image.'

Lila shifted on her chair.

'In what way?' She cradled her mug between her hands, her appetite gone.

'She had hair the same lovely colour, looked exactly like you from behind and when I saw her face, she was so much like you she could have been a relative of yours.'

'Oh …' Lila felt dread coursing through her. 'That much like me, eh?'

'Yes. It was only the fact that she was wearing different clothes and didn't have a baby bump that convinced me she wasn't you. I mean … take away the pregnancy and stand you two next to each other and I'd be pushed to tell the difference.'

Roxie was clearly surprised at how much the woman had resembled Lila, but for Lila, this was something she didn't want to hear. *Ever.*

'I need to go to the toilet.'

Lila pushed her chair back and stood up slowly then crossed the café on wobbly legs. Why was it that just when everything seemed good, something had to go wrong?

12

JOANNE

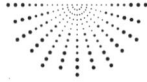

*J*oanne ran into the library, desperate to share her news with Max, but as she went through the double doorway, her baggy yoga top snagged on the door handle and she jerked forwards. The muffin she'd been holding flew through the air, sailing past the turnstile gate at the side of the counter. She stared in horror as it hit an elderly gentleman on the head, bounced off and hit his shoulder then landed on the carpeted floor.

He put the hardbacks he was holding on the counter and looked up as if thinking the muffin had fallen from the ceiling. At the same time, Max turned to the door, and seeing Joanne there, smirked then dropped his gaze to the books and started scanning them.

Joanne unhooked her top from the door handle, pushed her hair back behind her ears and strolled into the library as if she's just arrived and nothing had happened. She passed through the turnstile, head held high, trying not to giggle as she saw the elderly gent pick up the muffin and look around again. He clearly had no idea that it had come from Joanne and she hoped he wouldn't work it out.

She made her way to the romance section and pretended to browse the shelves while waiting for Max to come and speak to her.

When she felt his breath on her neck and smelt his familiar cologne, she turned to gaze into his dark brown eyes. It didn't matter how many times she looked at him, she still had butter-flies. Max was her boyfriend, he loved her, and they woke every morning in each other's arms. They were as close as two people could be and she hoped it would always be that way.

'So you're abusing the elderly people of Wisteria Hollow with muffins now, are you?' His eyes were filled with mischief.

Joanne snorted. 'I was in a hurry and my top caught on the door.'

'I like that top. I wish I could have come to yoga with you and watched you in all those bendy poses.'

'Max!' She glanced around them. 'You can't say things like that when you're at work.'

'You're right. Imagine if someone overheard.' He took his glasses off and wiped them on the hem of his shirt then put them back on. 'It doesn't help that my glasses mist up when I'm near you.'

Joanne smiled but heat filled her cheeks. 'Really?'

'You're very hot, Joanne, don't you realise?'

He brushed her cheek with his fingers and the flush in her cheeks spread as a familiar heat emanated through her body.

'I love that you see me like that.'

'How else would I see you?'

'You're the best.' She grinned at him. 'Oh … I almost forgot. I have some news.'

'Good news?'

'Yes. Otherwise, I wouldn't have been rushing and overarm bowled that rather delicious muffin. Such a waste.'

'Were you bringing it for me?'

She nodded, although she hadn't thought that initially when she'd grabbed it at the café, but now realised she'd have left it for Max for his break.

'Damn shame as it's in the bin under the counter now.' He grimaced.

'I'll go and get you another one.'

'You're my favourite girlfriend.'

'Don't tease me like that. I'd better be your only girlfriend.'

'You are.'

Joanne swayed from side to side as she admired him. He was just gorgeous.

'So what's the news?'

'Oh! Right … well, I was at the café with Lila and Roxie and we were discussing the cottage and I told them how much we love it and want it and how disappointed we'll be if we don't get it and …'

'And?' Max was clearly tense now. His shoulders and eyebrows had risen and he drummed his fingers against his thighs.

'Bridget said we can have it.'

'What?'

Joanne nodded. 'She has to confirm some things with her solicitor, but she wants to accept our offer. She said something about her mum wanting us to have it and look after her garden and to raise children there.'

'This is brilliant!'

'I know!'

He wrapped his arms around her waist and lifted her up then swung her around. 'We have a home, Joanne, a home of our own.'

Joanne laughed and held him tight, delighted by his happiness but terrified he might drop her or let her go as she'd end up flying into one of the shelves.

'We do, but she does have to confirm it all first. This is the first stage, obviously, but she likes our offer and likes us, so it's all good.'

Max put her down gently then cupped her face and held her gaze.

'This is a very good sign, Joanne. I know you're right to advise caution and I will try not to pin all my hopes on this just in case, but if we had that cottage and that garden, it would be wonderful. We can raise a family there and have parties and read in the garden and … I could even manage, perhaps, to write there.'

'Of course you could. The snug would make a lovely study and in the fine weather you could write in the garden under the apple trees.'

'We could have a dog.' He smiled. 'Or would you prefer a cat?'

'I'd like both.'

'The commute to work is minimal.' He laughed.

'It is, and what we save on travelling expenses, we have to spend on the mortgage instead.' Joanne's stomach was fizzing so much she felt like she might burst.

'Thanks for coming to let me know.'

'Do you think I could have waited until the end of the day to tell you at home?'

'Probably not.'

They grinned at each other, as excited as little children on Christmas morning, then Max pulled her into a hug. As her face pressed against the crook of his neck, she breathed him in. This man was her friend, her lover and her future. Everything from here on in was about them and their partnership. They would move forwards together in whatever direction that took them, and it felt wonderful to have that security.

'Shall I pick up some champagne on my way home?' he asked. 'Or is it too soon to celebrate?'

Joanne shook her head. 'I think we can celebrate. Even if it's a tentative celebration for the cottage, we can still celebrate being in love and the life we have to share together.'

'Sounds good to me.' He kissed her hard enough to take her breath away then stepped back and adjusted his glasses. 'I'd better get back to work but if you do fancy dropping off another muffin later, that would be wonderful. I'm quite peckish now.'

'I'll drop another muffin off but only because you're so lovely.'

'Thank you. But this time, please don't hurl it at anyone, will you, or before we know it the village will soon be alive with the rumour that the library ceiling is raining baked goods.'

Joanne sniggered then kissed him quickly before walking away. The romance section of the library had plenty of passion and love within the covers of the books, but she couldn't believe that any of the stories were as delightful as her own.

13

LILA

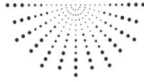

'Joanne, stop eating them or there won't be any left.' Lila wiped the sweat from her brow as she stood up. Joanne grinned at her, mouth and hands red from where she'd been picking strawberries then eating most of them. 'Seriously, Joanne, you've eaten more than you've picked.'

Almost two weeks had passed since Joanne and Max had their offer on Bridget's cottage accepted and Joanne hadn't stopped smiling.

'I can't help it.' Joanne licked her lips. 'They're just delicious.'

'I know that, but you're not supposed to eat them as they have to be weighed so we can pay for them *and* we need them for the party tomorrow.' Roxie shook her head, making her high ponytail sway.

'Gosh it's hot, isn't it?' Lila blinked behind her sunglasses.

'Have you drunk enough water?' Roxie asked.

'I've been trying to.'

'Well have some more and go and sit down under the tree where we left the cooler.'

'It's okay, I want to help you and Joanne.'

'And we want you to go and sit in the shade and have a drink.' Roxie folded her arms across her chest, showing that she meant business.

'Okay, then.' Lila shrugged. 'If you insist, but only because I'm responsible for this little one.' She pressed a hand over her belly, convinced that it was even bigger today than it had been yesterday. The denim maternity shorts she'd put on went under the bump while her pink stretchy vest top went over it and the colour really showed off her shape. Ethan had even said 'Wow!' when she'd got dressed that morning and so she'd left the cottage feeling really good about herself. She'd also promised to bring him some strawberries back but if Joanne kept eating them at this rate, Lila was worried there wouldn't be any left to share with Ethan.

A week tomorrow they were getting married and he intended on taking a week off afterwards to spend with Lila. They weren't having a honeymoon as such but intended on having some lie-ins and Netflix marathons, making the most of some time alone before two became three.

The strawberry fields were busy and people milled around the rows, carrying baskets and bowls that they filled with the sweetest, ripest fruit. Lila hadn't tasted one yet, in spite of the fact that her mouth had been watering at the delicious fragrance, because she knew that it was risky to eat unwashed fruit, especially in pregnancy. So while Joanne had been stuffing her face, Lila had sipped water and tried to ignore the urge to pop large, juicy strawberries into her mouth. Roxie had been very organised on their arrival and set their picnic cooler in a shady spot under the tree along with a blanket and some cushions, thus reserving a space for them to sit when they'd finished, and because, as she repeated several times, Lila was pregnant and should rest as soon as she felt the need.

Underneath the shade of the enormous oak tree, Lila kicked off her sandals and spread out the picnic blanket Roxie had packed then sat down and crossed her legs. She removed her sun hat and let the breeze cool her head while she waited for the throbbing in her legs to subside. Carrying the extra weight of the baby was getting harder to manage on her small frame and she wondered how she'd manage another eight to ten weeks. Surely, she'd get to the point where she'd pop? The image was awful so she shook it from her mind and focused instead on getting the picnic organised.

In the cooler were three more bottles of water, reusable bottles that Roxie had filled as part of her fight against plastic waste, and a wonderful selection of foods. Lila set them out in front of her, her mouth watering at the fat green olives, crusty bread, crumbly cheese, mini salmon and broccoli quiches, red grapes, roast chicken slices and selection of olive oil crisps. There was also a pot of clotted cream and an extra bottle of water that Lila assumed was to wash some strawberries so they could have them after the picnic.

When everything was laid out, she waved at Roxie and Joanne and they finished off picking, went and got their baskets weighed, paid for the strawberries then came to join her.

'This looks amazing, Lila.' Joanne sat on the blanket and stretched out her long legs.

'Roxie's the one we need to thank.' Lila shaded her eyes to look up at Roxie who was pushing her shoulders back.

'It's my pleasure and I'm delighted you're both pleased with the food.' She winced.

'You okay?' Lila asked.

'Yes, it's just a bit of backache from leaning over for so long. I can't get away with doing so much now I'm getting older.' Roxie winked.

'You're fitter than most twenty-year-olds, Roxie and you know it.' Joanne nudged her and they both laughed.

'Let's tuck in then because I'm starving.' Lila started to dish out the food onto the reusable picnic plates and Joanne handed out the forks while Roxie passed them the water bottles.

Half an hour later, Lila was full and relaxed. She was leaning against the trunk of the tree, hands resting on her belly, eyes closed. The leaves of the tree were gently rustling in the breeze, the air was sweet with the scents of strawberries and meadow flowers from surrounding fields and Roxie and Joanne were chatting away about their plans for the hen party the following day.

It was one of those perfect moments in life and Lila savoured every minute.

14

ROXIE

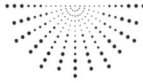

'It looks like everything's ready.' Fletcher gazed around their back garden at the round tables with parasols and cushioned chairs.

'It's wonderful, thank you.' Roxie leant her head on his shoulder. 'I don't know what I'd do without you.'

The day of Lila's garden party AKA hen party had arrived and Roxie felt like she would burst with excitement.

'Ditto,' he said as his kissed her forehead. 'And now you want me to make myself scarce, I guess?'

She laughed. 'You don't have to.'

'Well, I did say that I'd go to the pub for a pint with Ethan, Max, Rex, and Finlay. I think a few other blokes are going too.'

'Ah, I see ... so Ethan is having a stag do?'

'I don't think it's really a stag do as such. More a pint or two and a packet of cheese and onion crisps.'

'You go and have fun.'

'You're not having a stripper and wild party games, are you?' He pursed his lips.

'Ha! As if. The hen is heavily pregnant, I'm happily married and Freda Morris and Hilda Baker are coming. Can you imagine a hot, sweaty hunk gyrating around the begonias?'

'Being chased by Glenda and Stinky?' His lips curled upwards.

'Exactly.'

'Well, if you do need a hot dancer, let me know. I'll happily oblige.' He licked his lips, tousled his hair and shimmied in a circle.

'You, my love, are dancing for no one except me.' She pulled him close and slid her arms around his waist. 'Do you think I'd let the women of Wisteria Hollow ogle your … charms?'

Fletcher's cheeks flushed and he smiled. 'You still see me like that?'

'I do. I love and adore you and fancy you more than ever.'

'You took the words right out of my mouth.'

He kissed her, softly at first then with growing urgency, and a moan escaped her lips.

The doorbell ringing made them break apart like embarrassed teenagers.

'Can we continue that later?' Fletcher asked, his voice husky.

'I'd be very disappointed if we didn't.' Roxie glanced downwards. 'I think I'd better answer the door though. You'll scare someone away with that pants tent.'

Fletcher followed her gaze and laughed. 'I'll dash upstairs before you let your guests in and freshen up, then I'll head to the pub.'

Roxie followed him through to the hallway and watched him climb the stairs, then she opened the door with one hand while trying to hold two small and enthusiastic dogs back with the other.

～

AN HOUR LATER, all the guests had arrived and Roxie was milling around filling glasses with pink champagne and exchanging pleasantries with some of the women from the village. She'd received plenty of compliments on how well the fresh strawberries went with the champagne and on her beautiful garden. The roses she'd cut and set as centrepieces filled the air with their sweet, heady scent and she was pleased she'd suggested having the hen, or – as Lila liked to refer to it – *garden party* here.

Glenda and Stinky were behaving well and only scrounging a bit. Glenda had a keen eye for an easy target and wandered around the garden, sniffing out dropped morsels or waiting in front of women who seemed most likely to share their food. Stinky followed her closely, as always, and usually managed to get her fair share.

'This is going well,' Joanne said as she accepted a top up from Roxie.

'I think so. Do you think Lila's enjoying it?'

'Definitely.'

They looked at their friend who was sitting on a large garden chair with her feet up on a stool, a glass of lemonade in one hand and a bowl of strawberries in the other. Her skin was glowing, her hair shone and she had a beatific expression on her face that reminded Roxie of a painting she'd once seen of the *Madonna and child* in a gallery. Pregnancy had brought hormones and nausea and a changing shape to Lila but it also brought a serenity that suited her beautiful features. Roxie couldn't wait to see Lila holding her child and the thought made her eyes sting.

'Time for a speech?' Joanne asked.

'Okay.' Roxie nodded, sniffing.

'Are you going to do it?'

Roxie met Joanne's gaze. 'Me?'

'Well … you are, almost, the mother of the bride. Or the big sister at least.'

'I guess so … but you're like a sister to her too.'

'You're more articulate than I am.' Joanne smiled, her rosy cheeks like pink apples.

'I'm not sure that's true but I don't mind saying a few words, but could you get another bottle and fill glasses then?'

'No problem.'

Joanne headed to the fridge and Roxie took a swig of her champagne then went to the buffet table and picked up a spoon. She tapped it carefully on her glass and the garden fell silent, except for the singing of the birds in the trees.

'Ladies, thank you all for coming. As you know, next Saturday, our lovely Lila is getting married. It's a union we all want to celebrate and something that gives me so much joy in my heart. Lila has been a good friend of mine for quite some time and I see her as family. She's like the daughter, or sister, I never had and I love her dearly. To see Lila and Ethan so happy together and with a beautiful baby on the way is just incredible. I'd like you to raise your glasses to this kind, caring and beautiful woman and to her glorious future! To Lila, Ethan and a lifetime of happiness.'

Glasses were raised and 'to a lifetime of happiness' echoed around the garden, then one by one, the women went to Lila and hugged her, pressed gentle hands to her bump after asking permission, and spoke words of encouragement. It was a moment of female solidarity and celebration and Roxie was proud to be part of it.

15

LILA

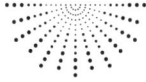

*I*t had been a wonderful afternoon and Lila had enjoyed herself immensely. Roxie had put on delicious food, the champagne had flowed – for everyone else – and Lila had enjoyed listening to the many anecdotes about how the other women met their partners and about their wedding days. Some had tales of perfection about their relationships where love at first sight had deepened into contentment and equal partnership, while others told tales of how things go could wrong on a wedding day – something Lila had experienced first-hand. The general message Lila took away from the stories was that as long as she went with the flow on her wedding day and didn't expect perfection, then nothing could ruin it.

The other guests had gone and Lila had hung back to offer to help Roxie tidy up but she had refused to allow Lila to lift a finger, insisting that it was Lila's party and she'd not allow it. Joanne said the same and then they ushered her to the door with a bag of strawberries, cake and sandwiches to take home for Ethan's dinner.

'Thank you again. I'm so grateful.' Lila hugged Roxie then Joanne. 'You've been so kind.'

'No problem at all. I'm just glad you enjoyed yourself.'

'I'm so glad you didn't get a stripper or anything like that.' Lila smiled. 'I'd have been mortified.'

'It's not really your style or mine, is it?' Roxie shook her head.

'Nor mine,' Joanne chipped in. 'Although having said that …'

The three of them laughed.

'Anyway, I'll take these home for Ethan and get an early night, I think. All the fresh air and good food, as well as this little one tap-dancing on my bladder have made me tired.'

'Have a good sleep and build your energy. This time next week you'll be a married woman.'

Lila's stomach did a loop the loop.

'I can't believe it.'

'It's so exciting!' Roxie bobbed up and down on the spot.

'Everything's perfect right now.' Lila sighed with contentment.

'Uh … Lila.' She turned to find Fletcher standing on the doorstep. 'Everything go okay?'

'Wonderfully. It was such a lovely afternoon. The food and company were amazing and—'

'Good. That's good.'

'Thank you so much for helping Roxie get everything organised.'

'No problem at all. Uh … Lila. I … uh …' Fletcher's face was contorting as if he was in pain.

'What is it?' She peered curiously at him and Roxie stepped past her and stared at her husband's face.

'Fletcher? Is something wrong?' Roxie asked.

'Kind of. See, I was about to make my way home and … I bumped into someone.'

'Who?' Lila and Roxie asked together.

'Someone who really wants to speak to you, Lila. I don't know how to explain so it's easier if I just bring her inside.' Fletcher turned and called out, 'You can come here now.'

A figure emerged from behind the garden hedge and Lila, Roxie, and Joanne gasped. It was the last person Lila expected to see and as her legs gave way, she felt strong hands grip her elbows and then everything went hazy.

∼

'LILA?'

'Yes.'

'Lila … open your eyes for me.'

Lila's eyelids fluttered and she opened her eyes and looked around. She was in Roxie's lounge on the sofa and Roxie was on the floor by her side.

'Are you all right?' Roxie's eyes were filled with concern.

'I'm okay.' Lila did a quick body scan. 'I think. What happened?'

'You were leaving … Fletcher arrived home … but he had someone with him.'

Lila frowned as she pictured leaving Roxie's then she sat upright. 'Roxie, I'm so sorry … I faked fainting.'

'Lie down, sweetheart.'

'Honestly. I faked fainting because I panicked and didn't know what else to do.'

'You faked it?'

'Yes.'

'So you're okay?'

'I'm fine. A bit shaken but I'm not ill.'

'What if Fletcher hadn't been there to catch you?'

'I wouldn't have fallen all the way … just swooned a bit.'

'Lila, I was terrified you were ill.'

'I'm so sorry, Rox, but seeing *her* … it just sent me into a spin and I did feel faint even if I didn't actually faint. I just wanted to get away from her.'

'I still think you should lie there for a bit longer.'

'Where is she?'

'In the back garden with Fletcher.'

'I can't believe she's here.' Lila rubbed her eyes.

'I don't think anyone can.' Roxie was wringing her hands. 'I mean … you never told us about her.'

'I'm sorry but it's really complicated. How did she find me?'

'Lila, I have no idea, but anyway … all that can wait. Our priority now is getting you checked out to make sure you and the baby are okay. Joanne has gone to get Ethan and Fletcher's going to call the GP once he's settled *her* outside.'

'I'm fine, honestly. Please don't call the doctor. I promise I didn't faint. I could use some water though.'

'I'll get you some but you need to take it easy. You've had a shock.'

Lila touched her belly. 'Would it have hurt the baby?'

'You didn't fall or bump yourself so I'm sure everything will be fine but you should rest anyway.'

'I need to see *her*.'

'It would be best to wait for a bit, wouldn't it? I better go and tell Fletcher not to call the doctor.'

The doorbell rang through the house and Roxie got up. 'I'm going to see who that is then get you that water, but you have to stay right there. Even if it was a *fake* faint, then you can deal with the rest afterwards.'

Lila nodded, knowing that Roxie was right, but it didn't stop the churning in her belly or the pounding of her heart. She had to calm down for the baby's sake because she needed to avoid stress but seeing Milly walking up Roxie's driveway had been the last thing she'd expected and it had knocked her sideways.

16

ETHAN

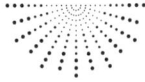

*E*than ran to Roxie and Fletcher's house, his heart racing, his palms cold and clammy in spite of the sun's warmth. Joanne had come to him and told him that Lila had fainted. He'd felt like the sky had fallen in and been catapulted back through time to when Tilly had been unwell. Losing Tilly had been the worst thing he'd been through and the idea of losing Lila too terrified him. He'd been able to keep it together by constantly reassuring himself that Lila was fit and healthy, strong and resilient, but was she? If she'd fainted like that, was she ill? Would he lose her and the baby?

He felt like crying and screaming, like pummelling the cars he passed with his fists then running a marathon so he'd feel only the pain in his body and not the agony in his heart. Lila and the baby were his world and he knew he'd die without them.

'Hey, Ethan … it's okay,' Roxie said as she opened the door to him then placed a cool hand on his arm. 'Lila's fine. She had a shock that made her feel faint but she didn't actually faint.'

'What shock? I thought she was having a lovely party? She sent me a text saying how wonderful the afternoon had been.'

'Joanne didn't tell you what happened?'

'No. Just that Lila had fainted.'

'Right. Well … there was a reason why she felt a bit faint and it wasn't anything to do with her health declining.'

'There was?' His skin was ashen, his forehead lined, and she could have sworn he'd aged twenty years since she'd last seen him.

'Come on in and see her for yourself.'

She ushered him inside and Ethan pushed his hands through his hair feeling as though he'd like to tear it out. He'd give anything just to see for himself that Lila was all right.

'She's in the lounge. I'll just go and get her some water.'

Ethan nodded then entered the lounge, trying to brace himself to be strong for his fiancée.

'Ethan?' Lila was on the sofa with her feet up, her head on one of Roxie's large colourful cushions.

'Lila!' In spite of his desire to stay calm he needed to hold her and to reassure himself that she was fine. He knelt next to the sofa and took her hands, felt the warmth of her skin and the bones beneath it, the pulse in her wrists.

'I'm all right, Ethan.'

'Are you sure?'

'Definitely. I'm so sorry you were scared but Joanne dashed off and I didn't have a chance to stop her. I didn't really faint.'

'Roxie said that, but Joanne came to get me and told me you'd collapsed. I left her standing there and raced over here. I was … terrified that something had gone wrong.' His voice broke and he pressed his face to Lila's hands, breathing in her scent, holding on to her as if to stop her leaving him.

'Ethan … please look at me.'

He raised his head and met her eyes. She gently removed one of her hands from his and stroked his cheek. 'I'm not ill. I was shocked to see someone … and I didn't know how to react so I faked a faint. It was stupid of me and incredibly irresponsible but I'd never have actually fallen to the ground. As it was, Fletcher caught me and brought me in here.'

'You really are okay?'

'I am.'

'Thank goodness! I don't know what I'd do if I lost you or the baby.'

'I'm here, my angel.'

He leant closer and rested his head gently on her bump and felt reassured when the baby moved as if knowing he was there.

'I'd do anything to protect you both.'

'I know you would and I love you for it.'

'Who was it that surprised you?'

Lila pressed her lips together until they went white. 'I'm so sorry Ethan but I have something I need to tell you. It's something I never told anyone before, something I hoped I could leave in my past and never have to face again. But … it seems that the past always catches up with you in one way or another.'

He watched her beautiful face, traced the outline of her jaw with his eyes, her smooth skin, her blonde hair. Whatever she had kept from him didn't matter because she was his world. He would listen and accept what she had to tell him without judgement or blame. It couldn't be worse than losing her would be.

'So tell me. Let me in, Lila. I want to know.'

She nodded and sat up then crossed her legs in front of her and Ethan sat at her side, taking her hand in both of his.

17

LILA

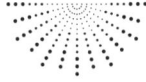

*L*ila felt terrible for worrying poor Ethan. When he entered the lounge, he looked distraught. She wished she could take the past hour back and stand there and be strong but she really had panicked and acted a bit rashly, which she wanted to blame on hormones but she knew part of it was fear. She'd come to Wisteria Hollow and created a new life for herself, had everything she could have wished for now, so having part of her not so happy past appear at her hen party was not something she'd expected in a million years.

And yet ... Hadn't her friends mentioned recently that they'd seen someone like her around the village? Why hadn't she let that fact sink in? It seemed so far-fetched that she hadn't given it too much thought and now here she was having to deal with her ignorance. Or had it been deeper than that, and she'd not wanted to accept that Milly was here?

'You're worrying me more now, Lila.' Ethan was gnawing at a cuticle, his eyes wide with concern.

'I'm so sorry, Ethan. I was just thinking about how to explain myself, but I guess it's just better to get it all out as quickly as possible.'

'Please do.'

'Have you seen Milly yet?'

'Who's Milly?'

'The woman who came to the door with Fletcher.'

He shook his head. 'Roxie said she's in the garden.'

At that moment, Roxie came in with a glass of water and a plate of biscuits. She looked from Lila to Ethan and back again.

'I'll leave you to it.'

'Stay.' Lila held out a hand. 'Please. I want you to hear this too.'

'Are you sure? I don't want to intrude.'

'How could you be intruding, Roxie? You're my best friend.'

Roxie nodded and perched on the coffee table, eyes wide, hands clasped in her lap. 'Okay then.'

Lila sucked in a deep breath. 'Milly's my sister.'

'She's your spitting image,' Roxie said.

'She's my identical twin.'

'You have a twin?' Ethan half rose from the couch then sank back down again. 'A twin sister?'

'Yes. Milly. She's my twin.' She repeated it as if to try to get it to sink in and because she was buying time to tell them the rest.

'A twin.' Roxie was blinking rapidly and she was scratching at her head. 'Wow.'

'I'm so sorry I didn't tell either of you. It wasn't that I didn't want to, or intend not to, more that I thought I'd left that part of my life behind. You both know what my parents were like, how they weren't bothered about me at all and it was the same with Milly.' She sipped the water Roxie had brought her, remembering how awful her childhood had been making her mouth dry, making her feel queasy.

'When did you last see her?' Ethan asked.

Lila frowned. 'Years ago. It was in the early days of my relationship with Ben … and so it must be around eight … maybe nine years ago. The years have passed so quickly that I find it hard to keep track.'

'That's a long time,' Roxie said.

'I know.'

'Didn't she try to contact you before?' Ethan shifted his position slightly.

'We had a furious argument about our parents. She wanted to give them another chance, but I didn't. I said that they weren't bothered about knowing either of us, that they didn't care if we were happy and healthy or even alive half the time, and that we should put it all behind us. Milly struggled badly with their rejection and neglect more than I did, I guess. Or perhaps it was because I was so besotted with Ben by that point that I felt they didn't matter anymore. I had someone to love me.' She glanced at Ethan. 'Sorry. It doesn't change how I feel about him.'

'Ben is an utter bastard!' Roxie tutted. 'A complete and utter waster.'

Ethan smiled briefly. 'I know how you feel about him.' He nodded. 'I don't feel threatened.'

'Good.' Lila squeezed his hand. 'I never loved him like I love you.'

'Did he know about her?' Ethan peered up at her from behind his lashes and Lila's heart squeezed.

'No. I kept her a secret because I was going to surprise him by turning up for a date with her tagging along, but then we argued, and I was so angry with her because I felt like she was taking our parents' side that I just didn't. And time went on and it seemed ridiculous to tell him. I thought he'd think I was mad or weird for not saying anything up to that point. Plus, I had such a bad taste in my mouth from how my parents behaved that her rejection on top of theirs made me feel like I was damaged and the last thing you want a new lover to see you as is damaged. I mean, what does it say about someone when even their closest family members don't give a damn about them? It's hurtful, embarrassing and humiliating. It makes it very difficult to value yourself and I was worried it might make other people … like Ben … see me as worthless too.'

'I can understand that.' Ethan bobbed his head. 'But you are a wonderful person and it breaks my heart to think of you feeling that way.'

'Mine too,' Roxie said, nodding.

'Milly became a secret part of my past. I didn't want to resurrect the pain, so I buried her deep in my mind and forgot about her, or at least I thought I had. She sometimes resurfaced in my dreams but that was all. Only … since I became pregnant, she has come into my mind again. I guess I've wondered what she's doing and how she is, thought about how I'd answer if our child ever asks if I have any siblings.'

'How did she find you though?' Ethan was gazing into the cold fireplace now, as if he could find the answer there.

'I think I might know.' Lila sighed. 'When I found out I was pregnant, I had this overwhelming urge to find out more about my ancestry. I couldn't ask my parents, obviously, so I ordered one of those DNA kits.'

'Those things are fascinating.' Roxie was leaning forwards with her hands on her knees.

'I'm assuming that Milly must have done one recently and was therefore able to track me down.'

'But how would she have found out where you lived?' Ethan asked. 'Surely you didn't post your contact details on there as public?'

'Not exactly, but I did put my location on there. I think she's been in the village for a few weeks so she must have checked things like phone listings and more, put two and two together then possibly asked around. It's even possible she saw me in the village but didn't like to approach me until she felt sure she'd seen me. Or she could have been finding out about my life.'

'It's a bit creepy sounding.' Roxie gave a dramatic shudder.

'In some ways I guess it does sound a bit creepy but I suspect she was just keen to find me.'

'Could it have been that twin thing that led you both to do a DNA ancestry test?' Ethan's eyes were wide.

Lila shrugged. 'We had that twin communication link you read about when we were younger but it seemed to wear off as we grew up. However, perhaps the pregnancy kick started it again or something. I'm not sure.'

'Some things just can't be explained.' Roxie cleared her throat. 'I've watched some documentaries on things like this and even though, as a species, we'd like to explain everything, we simply can't. It could have been a twin thing, it could have been fate, it could have been coincidence. However, what matters now is whether or not you're strong enough to deal with this. We can always tell her to go away.'

Lila smiled at Roxie then at Ethan.

'No, don't do that. This is like the final piece of my puzzle and it's high time I spoke to Milly and addressed our issues. Whether we can work things out or have to go our separate ways for good, at least I'll have tried. I owe her that much, but I also owe it to myself.'

'Do you want to speak to her now or leave it until tomorrow?' There was a tiny line between Ethan's brows that seemed to be getting deeper by the minute.

'I'll do it now. Outside though because I need some air. Is that all right, Roxie? I don't want to take over your garden.'

'Don't be silly, Lila. My garden is your garden. I'll make a pot of tea and take it out for you.'

Roxie left them alone and Lila looked at Ethan.

'I'm so sorry I didn't tell you before.'

'You don't need to be. This was clearly a difficult thing for you to deal with and I know how hard it can be to resurrect things from your past. Life can be painful when people you love don't feel the same or when you lose them, whether to disease and death or just to their stubborn mindedness. I'm sure Milly struggled too but the fact that she's come here now shows that she wants to see you.'

'It does.'

'Do you … want to speak to her alone or do you want me with you?'

Lila swallowed. She didn't want to hurt Ethan but she also didn't know what Milly was thinking or feeling.

'If it's okay with you, I'll speak to her alone first. Only because she doesn't know you and because I don't want her to feel we're ganging up on her. Then, once we've spoken, I can introduce you properly.'

'Sounds good to me.'

'I love you so much, Ethan.'

'And I love you.'

They kissed then got up and went out to the kitchen. Ethan took a seat at the breakfast bar next to Fletcher but Lila felt his eyes on her as she went to the back door and knew that if he could protect her just by looking at her, he would do. She lifted her chin, pushed her shoulders back and headed outside into the beautiful evening to speak to the twin she'd once shared a womb with, the sister who'd once been her closest friend and the woman who she hadn't seen in years.

18
LILA

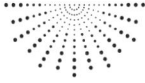

In the garden, Milly was sitting at one of the tables. Her hair was loose and shiny, her profile achingly familiar, with the same straight nose, slightly rounded forehead and small chin as Lila. She was slouched forwards, her hands holding a glass of water on the table in front of her, gazing into space.

Lila went to the table and sat opposite her sister then summoned her courage and met Milly's eyes.

They stared at each other. As children, they'd done this for hours, mirroring each other's gestures, repeating each other's words. It had irritated their mother and she'd often told them to stop, but when she left them alone again they'd return to their game. Back then, they'd had a deep bond, one that Lila realised she had missed and yet forced herself to surrender so she could get on with her life.

Their eyes roamed the features that were identical and it was like looking into a mirror. The only difference between them had been a small mole on Milly's left shoulder. Now, of course, there was a big difference – Lila was pregnant.

'Hello Milly.' Lila decided to break the silence, needed to break it.

'Lila.' Milly nodded.

'You're here.' It wasn't a question, more acceptance of the inevitable because Lila suspected that she'd always known deep down that Milly would turn up one day.

'I've been searching for you for a while. A few months ago, I had an overwhelming urge to take one of those DNA tests that trace your ancestry.'

Lila nodded. 'Me too.'

Milly raised her eyebrows. 'You think it was because of the pregnancy?'

'I wanted to know if I had any relatives out there and to find out more about our ancestors because I couldn't ask … *them* about it.'

'So you haven't seen our parents recently?'

'Not for years.' Lila pressed her lips together. 'Have you?'

Milly shook her head. 'Same.'

'They wouldn't want to know if I did try to contact them.'

'About the baby?'

Lila shrugged.

'They might, Lila.'

'And what would be the point? Nothing would ever be what they expected or hoped or wished for, and I won't have my child being another disappointment for them. I can't bear it. We were … an inconvenience … and I don't want that seeping back into my life now.'

'Are things good for you?'

'Yes.'

Milly smiled. 'I'm glad.'

'Are you?'

'Of course, I am. I know we argued back then but I never hated you. I've missed you desperately, but I honestly thought you wouldn't want to see me.'

'For a while I didn't. Then I tried not to care.'

'Are you angry I came searching?'

'I'm … really happy you're here, Milly.' And then, a lump rose in Lila's throat and she was unable to say more.

'Oh Lila, don't cry.' Milly jumped up and came round the table to Lila then crouched at her side. 'I'm so sorry I didn't try to find you sooner.'

Lila covered her eyes with her hands.

'I should have, I know. What I said back then was cruel and I didn't mean it. I was just angry, and I took it out on you.'

Milly touched Lila's arm and it was like an electric shock, as if her skin recognised Milly's. She lowered her hands and looked down into her twin's face.

'Thank you for coming.'

Milly smiled. 'I know we've got a lot to talk about and I also know that it will take time for us to become … *friends* again

… but I do love you. I always loved you. And now you're having a baby. It's amazing, Lila.'

She reached out as if to touch Lila's bump then paused, her hand in mid-air.

'It's okay.' Lila nodded and Milly rested her hand gently on Lila's belly. Beneath her touch, the baby responded making them both giggle.

'Hello baby. I'm your aunt and I can't wait to meet you.'

∼

LILA AND MILLY sat in the garden and talked for over an hour. Roxie popped out with water for them and Ethan waved from the kitchen just to let Lila know he was there if she needed him. She was grateful for their support but also glad to have the time to spend alone with Milly. She'd heard stories about family estrangement, read websites that advised people on how to deal with it, and yet she'd thought she was doing quite well. She had believed that she was managing not seeing her family, and to a certain extent she was. She was sad that her parents weren't different and that they had never cared, but her deep grief had lain with the gap in her life left by Milly's absence. It was why she'd tried so desperately to push Milly from her mind, so far from her conscious thoughts that she emerged only in dreams.

And here they were, together again, and the walls of ice that had risen up between them the last time they'd spoken were melting. It was like they'd never been apart, never felt such anger towards each other. Of course, Lila knew it would take time to rebuild their relationship, and part of her was somewhat hesitant to fully commit to it after so long, especially when she was pregnant and had a better life now, but at the same time, she knew Milly and wanted to give this a chance. Surely their relationship deserved that chance?

'I'm getting married next Saturday,' Lila said.

'That soon? I knew about the wedding because Fletcher told me that the men were holding Ethan's stag party when I saw them outside the pub. But he didn't tell me when it was. A baby *and* a wedding though. Goodness, Lila, you've so much going on.'

'I know.' Lila smiled. 'Will you come?'

'Oh no … I wouldn't want to intrude.'

'You're my twin and I'd like you there. But … I do understand if it's too much too soon.'

'I'd like to come. As long as you're sure?'

'I am.'

'I have to go away for a few days first because of my job, but I can come back for Saturday.'

Lila nodded. Milly was a travel writer and she'd been all over the world since they last spoke. It was an exciting career and Milly enjoyed it, but she'd also confessed that keeping moving was her way of trying to deal with her pain. She'd tracked Lila down via the ancestry website and visited Wisteria Hollow several times over recent weeks, hoping she'd catch sight of Lila. Then she had done but she'd been hit by nerves and unable to speak to Lila when she'd seen her with Ethan and spotted her bump, worried that if she spoke to her, Lila would panic. It had taken her a few visits to pluck up the courage to do anything, and then seeing Ethan and his friends outside the pub that afternoon had made her realise that it was now or never. When it had looked like

Fletcher was leaving, Milly seized the chance to speak to him alone.

On seeing Milly, Fletcher had been struck dumb. She'd asked him not to introduce her to Ethan until she'd spoken to Lila because she didn't know if her sister's fiancé even knew of her existence. That was why Fletcher had brought her straight to Lila, leaving Ethan and the others behind.

They exchanged phone numbers and Lila gave Milly details about the wedding venue.

'I'd better be going. I have a flight to Cyprus later and I need to pack.'

'Where are you staying?'

Milly gave a sad smile. 'I have a small flat in Slough that I use as a base because it allows me easy access to Heathrow but I'm rarely there. As I said, I keep moving.'

'I'd love to see some photos of the places you've been sometime.'

'It would be fabulous to show you because I have so many. I've been to some fantastic destinations as well as some awful ones.'

'Do you have a blog?'

'Yes. And I'm freelance so I write for several different magazines. It's really exciting. I'll send you a link to the blog so you can have a look.'

Lila walked with Milly to the house and in the kitchen she introduced her sister to Ethan and Roxie. She could see Ethan's eyes widen as he saw that Lila and Milly really were identical. It must be strange for him to see his fiancée's double and she tried to put herself in his place, wondering how she'd feel if things had been the other way around.

At the front door, she paused, not sure how to act, but Milly took her hand.

'You take care and ring me anytime.'

'And you'll be there next week?'

'I will. I'm looking forward to it.' Milly smiled then leant forwards and kissed Lila's cheek before walking down the driveway and disappearing behind the hedge.

Lila turned around and Ethan was right there, arms open, eyes watchful, as he waited to see how she was feeling. She stepped into his embrace and held him tight, needing his love and support more than ever and feeling grateful that he was there.

19

ROXIE

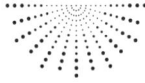

'*I* can't find my shoes!' Roxie bounded up the stairs, one hand on her heated rollers, the other holding her boobs in her strapless bra. 'Fletcher! Have you seen my shoes?'

Fletcher was standing in their bedroom, a smile playing on his lips, holding a pair of nude heeled sandals in one hand and a purple tie in the other.

'You've got them?' She shook her head.

'They were on the bed, Rox, where you left them.'

'I didn't see them there.'

'That's because you pulled the duvet back looking for your earrings then covered your shoes.' His voice was calm and she knew he was trying not to rile her because she'd been in a panic since she woke early that morning.

Roxie took the shoes from him and put them on but he started to laugh.

'What's so funny?'

'You're not going like that are you?'

Roxie looked down at herself and grimaced. She wasn't even dressed yet and could see his point. 'I thought this was a good look.'

'You look wonderful in that sexy underwear, but I don't think you should walk Lila down the aisle in a lacy bra and thong, Rox.'

'You're totally right. Can you imagine?' She shuddered. 'Will you help me into my dress?'

'As long as you can help me with my tie.'

He lifted the hanger with her purple silk dress from the mirror and unzipped it then held it out as Roxie stepped into it. She turned for him to zip the dress and shivered with desire as his hands brushed against her skin. He placed his hands on her shoulders and pressed his lips to her nape, his breath tickling the sensitive skin of her hairline. When he stepped away, she exhaled slowly as she willed her longing for him to drift away. Now was not convenient.

'Shall I do your tie for you?'

He nodded. 'Please.'

She hooked it around his collar then deftly looped it around and slid it up to his throat before smoothing its length against his shirt.

'I just need to take my rollers out and grab my bag then we can go.'

'The girls are ready downstairs,' he said. 'They look incredibly cute in their ruffs.'

'I just hope they behave today.'

'They will. I have a feeling that they're aware it's an important day and they both adore Lila and Ethan.'

'They do, don't they?'

'I'll go and let them out one more time before we leave.'

Roxie sat in front of her dressing table mirror and started to remove her rollers. She looked at her reflection, at her flawless make-up, beautiful silk dress and freshwater pearl necklace and bracelet that Fletcher had got her for Christmas. As she removed the final roller, she realised that her hands were shaking. Today was such a big day for Lila and she wanted everything to go well for her.

She combed through her hair with her fingers then closed her eyes and took some slow deep breaths, trying to release the nerves and to harness the calm control that she wanted today.

Everything was planned.

Everything was ready.

Everything was good.

It was going to be a very special day.

20

LILA

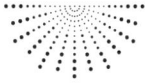

*T*his was it then.

Today was the day …

Lila had showered and washed her hair, blow-dried it, mois-turised from top to toe with a silky body butter that smelt like vanilla then painted her fingernails. Ethan had painted her toenails for her last night after she'd become frustrated that she couldn't reach without straining because her bump got in the way. She could have gone to the beauty salon but knew she'd need some time alone this morning to calm herself. Ethan had stayed with her last night, as neither of them had wanted to be apart the night before their wedding as tradition might dictate, but he'd left two hours ago to get ready at his mother's home.

Now Lila was sitting in the lounge with Cleo and Willy either side of her on the sofa as if they knew that today was a big day for her. She ran her hands over their soft fur and allowed it to soothe her, let their deep contented purring seep into her and slow her heartbeat, ease the tension in her shoulders and steady her.

Lila's mind had been busy since she'd woken just after dawn. She'd gazed at Ethan's profile as he slept, wondering how he could rest when today was such a big day but also glad that he could. This was an important day for them both. Ethan had been married before and suffered the loss of his wife, so Lila had no doubt that his emotions would run high today for more than one reason. And for Lila herself, she'd been jilted by Ben and however hard she might try to push it away, there would be a ghost of that memory around today. However, she wouldn't allow it to ruin today. In fact, it would make today even better because if it hadn't happened then she wouldn't have met and fallen in love with Ethan and now be pregnant with their child, so today really was a day for rejoicing.

There was a knock at the front door then a creak as it swung open.

'Lila? It's me … Roxie … and Fletcher. Are we all right to come in?'

'Of course.'

Lila got up slowly, trying not to disturb the cats although she knew that when they saw Glenda and Stinky they'd soon stir.

'Oh sweetheart, you look so beautiful.' Roxie tottered over to her on nude sandals and hugged her. 'My beautiful, beautiful girl.'

'Don't, Rox. You'll set me off and my mascara will run. Plus, I'm still in my dressing gown.'

Roxie stood back and gazed at her; green eyes filled with love.

'I can't believe you're getting married today. Not because I'm shocked you've fallen in love but because it's come so quickly. Everything in the past year seems to have happened in a whirlwind.'

A growl from the doorway caught their attention. Fletcher stood there looking very smart in a grey suit with a tie the same purple as Roxie's dress. He held two leads in his hands and at the end of them were Glenda and Stinky wearing purple ruffs and looking incredibly cute. The growling was coming from Stinky who had locked eyes with Willy, while Glenda was backing out of the door, clearly wanting to avoid a confrontation with the cat at all costs.

'Morning, Lila. Exciting day today!' Fletcher smiled. 'Why don't I take these two on a walk around the village while you finish getting ready? I thought they'd be all right here, but clearly, while Glenda is still terrified of Willy, Stinky's prepared to fight for her honour.'

'It's up to you. The cats can go always go upstairs.' Lila nodded.

'No, it's no trouble. It's a beautiful morning and a walk will give these two the chance to use up some energy before the ceremony.'

'See you in a bit then Fletcher.' Roxie kissed him then he opened the front door. 'Make sure the girls don't get dirty.'

He laughed. 'I'll do my best.'

When they were alone, Lila sank onto the sofa and placed her hands on her trembling knees.

'Hey, you.' Roxie sat next to her and took her hand. 'It's all going to be fabulous today.'

'I know. I do know. I'm just ... nervous.'

'You're bound to be a bit anxious, but today you'll marry the man you love and seal the deal, then you can relax and prepare for your baby's arrival.'

Lila nodded. 'I think it's just the whole thing building, you know? The venue is incredible, the weather is just right and I'm hoping I don't let Ethan down in my home-made dress.'

'Darling, that dress is divine. Ethan will have his socks blown off when he sees you.'

Lila giggled. 'I hope not.'

'Well he'll have hearts in his eyes at least.'

'Do you have the flowers?'

'I do. They're in the hall ready. Everything's exactly as we planned.'

'Thank you so much.'

'It's my pleasure. Now let's get you dressed.'

Lila nodded. 'I'm ready.'

Roxie helped her up then led the way upstairs and Lila's heart lifted because Roxie was right: everything would be wonderful.

21

ETHAN

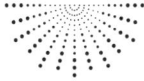

*E*than arrived at the vineyard an hour before the ceremony, wanting to check everything and have a chance to calm his nerves. He didn't know why he was nervous because he was about to marry the woman he loved, but still, his heart was thrumming and his mouth felt dry. His mum had come with him and she'd gone into the barn to greet some of the early arrivals and, knowing her, to ensure that everything looked as it should do.

'Everything all right?' It was Cesca, clad in a navy two-piece with a white blouse and navy court shoes. Her short dark hair was slicked down with some sort of gel and she looked calm and professional, making him think of a lawyer about to enter court.

'Yes, I'm good thanks. A bit nervous … not about getting married, but about … well, I'm hoping everything goes well.'

'That's perfectly understandable but don't you worry at all. That's why I'm here. All you have to do is turn up, which you've done, and marry the woman you adore. Easy, right?'

He nodded.

'Why don't you go for a wander? The vineyard is beautiful and a walk will soothe you then you can come back and await Lila's arrival.'

'That's a good idea, actually.'

'See you in thirty minutes.' Cesca checked her watch as if setting a timer then walked towards the barn, her clipboard tucked under her arm.

Ethan walked across the yard and let himself through a small gate, strolled past the large house then into a field. A path ran along the top near the hedge so he ambled along it, savouring the sweet air that smelt of grass and wild flowers. There were other notes to the scent too, like lychees, violets and pepper and he realised that it was coming from the vineyards that stretched out in front of him. Everywhere he looked, he saw green vines, brown fertile soil and ancient trees that towered over the fields like guards on duty.

His life had taken twists and turns he couldn't have predicted growing up but he was okay with it all. Lila's had been the same and he knew that she'd suffered her fair share of pain as well as someone else's too. The arrival of Milly had shocked her but also Ethan because he'd known nothing about Milly. Initially, his first feeling when he'd found out that Lila had a twin had been hurt. He'd felt betrayed because Lila hadn't told him about Milly, but when Lila had explained that she'd put her sister to the back of her mind with her past because it was too much to think about, he understood. Lila was his priority and though he could have ranted about her lying to him, he knew she hadn't done it consciously. Lila was a good person, gentle and kind and the fact that she'd buried Milly's existence deep in her heart had been for good reasons. Ethan

knew how much her parents had hurt her and losing Milly
must have been dreadful for her too. Families fell out,
parents left their children behind – his father had abandoned
him, after all – and siblings walked away from each other.
Sometimes, it was easier to let people go and pretend they'd
never existed than it was to admit to the fact that the relationship was damaged and painful and might never be fixed.
But as long as people were still alive, there was always a
chance that a way through the difficulties could be found.
For some, it would be too late, but for others there would be
time. Life was what it was, people were who they were and
sometimes being a blood relative just didn't mean you'd get
on well. Ethan hoped Lila and Milly could have a relationship now though, because he knew it would mean a lot to
Lila and that it would, hopefully, be good for her.

He gulped down the fresh air, letting nature calm him,
enjoying being outdoors on such a beautiful day. His
thoughts turned to Tilly, as they often did, and sent out a
silent message to her, wishing her well and telling her that he
hoped she was all right with what he was about to do. Once,
Tilly had been his world, but that awful disease had taken her
from him and then, Lila had come into his life. He'd thought
he'd never love again, never marry again but now he knew
differently. Grief was truly awful, but it meant that you loved
the person you'd lost, that you needed to adjust to not having
them in your life anymore. Ethan had grieved deeply for
Tilly and even now, even with everything he had, he missed
her. She'd been his friend as well as his wife and he knew
that a part of him would always miss her, but that didn't
detract from how much he loved Lila and their child. Things
were, he could believe now, as they were meant to be.

Something tickled his hand and he looked down to see a
ladybird, its red and black a contrast to his lightly tanned

skin. He raised his hand and watched as it crawled along, a tiny creature going about its business, oblivious to the fact that it had landed on a human being. Or at least he thought it was, but then, there was still much that human beings didn't know.

He blew on it gently and it opened its wings and flew away, disappearing quickly into the blue of the sky. Like Tilly, it had been there for a brief time, and yet it had been there, even if he could no longer see it. Something told him that Tilly was still there too, even if he could no longer see her, even if she only existed now in his heart and in his memories; she would always be a part of who he had been and who he had become.

2 2

ROXIE AND LILA

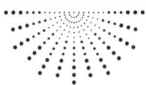

ROXIE

*T*he car pulled up in the vineyard car park and the
driver cut the engine.

'Thank you, Stuart.' Roxie smiled at the driver in the rear-
view mirror.

'My pleasure. Hope you have a wonderful day.'

Stuart was a former colleague of Fletcher's who'd taken early
retirement and set up a successful car sales business in
Surrey. It meant that he had a ready supply of cars in his
showroom and Fletcher had contacted him to ask if he had
anything that would make a good wedding car. Today he'd
turned up in a Rolls-Royce Silver Cloud and Lila had gasped
with delight as she left her cottage and Fletcher told her
she'd be going to her wedding in the fancy car.

'Thank you, Stuart.' Lila smiled then Roxie helped her out of
the back seat.

As Stuart drove away, Roxie smoothed Lila's dress down then tousled her softly waved hair before straightening the crown of flowers that Roxie had made for her using baby's breath, eucalyptus and cream roses. Set on Lila's blonde hair it looked beautiful, a lovely natural alternative to a tiara. And with the flowing dress and gold sandals, Lila looked every inch the boho summer bride.

'And here's the bouquet.' Roxie handed Lila the bouquet that Fletcher had carried in a box and Lila accepted it then lifted it to her face.

'The flowers smell incredible.'

'It matches your crown and your dress perfectly.'

'I'm so grateful.' Lila smiled and Roxie's heart squeezed.

'God, I love you, Lila.' She went to hug her friend then remember the bouquet so cupped Lila's face gently instead, taking care not to spoil her make-up.

'I love you too.'

'Right, you two,' Fletcher interrupted them. 'It's three minutes to two so we'd better get over to the barn or Ethan's going to start worrying.'

'Ready?' Roxie held out her arm.

'I'm ready.' Lila nodded then hooked her arm through Roxie's and they crossed the car park and headed for the barn.

Outside they stopped and Fletcher crouched down and adjusted the dogs' ruffs then gave each one a stroke. 'Be good for us, girls, and there will be treats for you later.'

Cesca appeared at the doorway and her eyes lit up.

'Lila you look exquisite! That dress is just perfect and you are literally glowing.'

'Thanks.' Roxie saw Lila's cheeks flush at the praise. 'I hope Ethan thinks so.'

'He will!' Cesca grinned. 'He's waiting for you. I'll just let the musicians know you're here.'

She ducked inside and Roxie and Lila took their place behind Fletcher. They couldn't see beyond him but she could hear voices then a hush as Cesca signalled to the musicians she'd employed.

This was it. It was going to happen. From the corner of her eyes she saw Lila straighten her shoulders and lift her chin.

∾

LILA

'LILA!'

She turned to see Milly hurrying towards her, holding a fascinator to her head with one hand and carrying a pair of pink heels in the other.

'I'm so sorry I'm late. Bloody taxi driver got lost.'

'It's okay. You're here now.'

Milly reached Lila's side and looked at her then her eyes filled with tears. 'Oh sis, you look gorgeous.'

Lila swallowed hard, the lump that had popped into her throat threatening to choke her. 'Thanks … for … coming.'

'Thanks for inviting me.'

They gazed at each other, communicating in ways only they could feel, then the opening bars of an instrumental version of Christina Perri's 'A Thousand Years' drifted out of the barn.

'We'd better go in soon,' Roxie whispered.

'I'll see you in there.' Milly nodded then kissed Lila's cheek before ducking inside.

'Am I ready to go then?' Fletcher asked.

'Let's do it.' Lila smiled.

Fletcher stepped through the doors, Glenda on one side, Stinky on the other and a collective gasp whispered through the air, followed by another as Roxie and Lila stood in the doorway. As they walked slowly along the aisle, Lila glanced at their guests and smiled, then fixed her eyes straight ahead, because there he was.

Ethan ...

The man she loved with all her heart.

23

ETHAN

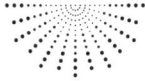

*E*than held his breath as the music started, only releasing it as Fletcher began his journey along the aisle. Glenda and Stinky trotted along next to him, looking as if they were proud to have such an important role at the wedding. Guests gasped at how cute the dogs were and Ethan couldn't help smiling.

Then Fletcher was at the front, standing next to him with the dogs, and Ethan's eyes moved to the doorway again.

And there she was.

Ethan felt a jolt to his chest. He'd always thought Lila was beautiful but today, her beauty was overwhelming. In a dress that seemed to flow from her frame, made of pale blue silk and chiffon, she resembled a fairy-tale princess. On her head was a crown of flowers and as she got closer, he saw that she'd embroidered flowers on the bodice and the hem of the gown. She held a bouquet of flowers that matched the crown and she held them just below her bump which was empha-sised by the cut of the gown that stopped just below her bust.

Ethan had seen pictures of woodland fairies and spirits and today Lila reminded him of them. She looked like a beautiful fecund woodland goddess and he was struggling to believe that she was walking towards him, that her eyes were fixed on him and him alone.

When she reached him, Roxie hugged her then took her bouquet and went to stand at the side. Ethan held out his hands and took Lila's and she smiled up at him. The music faded and for a moment, they stood frozen, lost in each other, then the registrar greeted them and the ceremony began.

It was over far too quickly, and yet not quickly enough, because Ethan was desperate to hold his new bride.

'Go on then,' the registrar, a man who reminded Ethan of Al Pacino, said. 'You can kiss now.'

Ethan slid his arms around Lila and stepped closer to her. She wound her arms around his neck, the bump between them, then Ethan lowered his head and kissed her. Around them, their friends and family clapped and cheered and Ethan felt a warm glow spread through him. He had everything he wanted and needed right here in his arms and he would do everything in his power to protect his wife and child. Life had dealt him a cruel blow but then life had given him more than he could have imagined having.

'Hello, wife,' he said.

'Hello husband.' Lila held his gaze, her eyes the blue of tropical waters, her skin the colour of peaches and cream, and her scent as sweet as vanilla.

'Here's to our life together,' he said as he took her hand then turned and smiled at their guests.

'Congratulations!' Roxie and Fletcher got to them first, hugging them and posing for photographs, then Ethan's mum and Lila's sister joined them and soon, the whole barn was filled with chatter and laughter and the band began to play again.

24

LILA

The day had passed in a blur and Lila was glad she'd taken Roxie's advice and paused at regular intervals to take mental snapshots. They had hired a local photographer and asked their guests to take lots of photos on cameras and smartphones but even so, the actual experience would only happen once, and Lila wanted to treasure it.

Darkness had fallen outside, but inside the barn, fairy lights twinkled from above them where they were wrapped around the wooden ceiling beams and supporting beams that ran to the floor, and votives glowed in the candleholders on the tables. The flowers Roxie had provided from her garden filled the barn with their fresh summery aroma and everywhere Lila looked, friends and family were smiling, laughing and celebrating.

She kept looking at the wedding ring nestled above her engagement ring and it made her feel cosy and warm, as if it had cemented what she had with Ethan. Being engaged had been wonderful but being married was something else altogether. Perhaps it was because of what she'd been through in the past, perhaps it was because as they'd said their vows she'd gazed into Ethan's eyes and known that he did love her with all of his heart, that he did mean it when he said he'd always be there for her and their family.

Lila had received lots of compliments on her dress and when she'd said that she'd made it herself, people had told her that she could make dresses and add them to her already successful online business. She'd been making crochet animals and baby clothes for a while now but the idea of adding wedding dresses and possibly bridesmaid dresses to that was quite exciting. However, she also knew that she had a busy time ahead and so she'd put the idea on hold for now as she prepared for the arrival of their baby and hopefully return to it in the not-too-distant future.

Milly had been lovely, sitting at a table with Joanne and Max through the reception then chatting to other guests as if she'd known them for years. She'd told Lila that when people had asked why they hadn't seen her before, she'd replied that she'd been travelling (not a lie) and that she'd been really busy, so getting to the village had been difficult. There was no point telling everyone the finer details about what had happened and everyone who'd asked had seemed happy to accept what she told them as a perfectly reasonable explanation for her absence from Lila's life. Some people might question why they hadn't been closer over the years, but others knew that families could be close or they could be distant, live in each other's pockets or be estranged. It was just a part of life. Now though, Milly had come back into Lila's life and she hoped it would stay that way. They had to take their time and get to know each other again but Lila felt hopeful for a good relationship and that her twin sister would be an aunt to her child.

Ethan had also been incredibly accepting of Milly's appearance. Lila would have understood if he'd been angry that she'd omitted to tell him about Milly, would have felt hurt had it been the other way around, and yet there had been no anger from him, no recriminations, just understanding and love. He seemed to accept that Lila had needed to push all thoughts of her twin from her mind and he hadn't judged her for it, and it made her love him even more. She could see how he would make an amazing father and be a calm and positive influence in their child's life – perhaps even children's lives.

'What are you smiling about?' Ethan asked as he nuzzled her ear.

'At how lucky I feel.'

She turned from watching the dancing to face him, her heart giving a leap at how handsome he was in his charcoal grey suit with the embroidered blue tie she'd made him to match her dress. He'd been curious when she'd handed him the package that morning, but he'd agreed not to open it until he was getting ready.

'I feel lucky too.' He kissed her. 'You know what's strange? This tie you made me, which is incredible by the way, has a ladybird on it.'

'Why's that strange?'

'This morning when I put it on, I didn't notice because I was so nervous all I could focus on was trying to stop shaking. I just saw how lovely the tie was and how well it went with my suit. I had no idea then that it would match your dress and I also missed the ladybird on it.' He ran a finger over the black and red embroidered creature. 'After I arrived at the vineyard, Cesca suggested I went for a walk to calm down. I did, and a ladybird landed on my hand. It just made me think about life and how we're all connected.'

Lila nodded. 'The ladybird symbolises good luck and love as well as taking time to evolve and change.'

'And we have changed, haven't we?'

'We have and I know that we'll continue to change and grow together. Also …' She licked her lips, not sure whether to say this to him but also not wanting to hold back. 'As I stitched the ladybird onto the tie, I was thinking of Tilly. I knew she'd be on your mind today and in some way, I wanted to acknowledge that she was here, just in a different form.'

'You're incredible, Lila. You never cease to amaze me.'

'I love you and want you to be happy.'

'I am happy and I know that Tilly would be happy for us. She had a good heart too.'

Lila nodded. 'Of course, she did.'

'Now … I know it's been a long day but how do you feel about one more dance?'

'I'd love to.'

He took her hand and led her onto the dance floor.

25

ROXIE

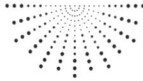

'*D*on't they make the perfect couple?'

Roxie rested her head on Fletcher's shoulder as they stood watching Lila and Ethan dancing. Glenda and Stinky lay at their feet, tiny heads on tiny paws, exhausted after all the excitement. The barn was beautiful, lit with tiny lights and candles, the dance floor quiet now except for the bride and groom and Joanne and Max as they slow danced around to LeAnn Rimes' 'How Do I Live?'

The wedding had been wonderful. Lila had looked like a princess straight out of a fairy tale and Ethan had been her handsome prince. Roxie could burst with how happy she was for them and the exciting year they had ahead of them. Christmas would be even more special with a baby around and Roxie was already thinking about what she could buy for the baby.

'They really do.' Fletcher entwined his fingers with Roxie's. 'Kind of like us.'

'We look good together?'

'I'd say so.' He nudged her.

'Me too.' She lifted her head and smiled up at him. 'I guess you just know when it's right.'

'And Joanne and Max too.' He nodded in their direction.

'It'll be them next.'

'You think they'll get married?'

'Definitely. Just look at how smitten they are.'

'It's like everyone's happy now.'

'For once.'

Fletcher laughed. 'Long may it last.'

Roxie spotted Milly across the other side of the barn talking to Freda. She was Lila's identical twin, and yet, she was different. Roxie hadn't said as much, but although Milly was physically identical to Lila, their mannerisms were different. Lila was gentler, more vulnerable, while Milly seemed somewhat tougher, more worldly, with something of an edge. Of course, she had been travelling for work, so that could be explained, but now that Roxie had been around them both for some time and seen them together, she thought she could tell them apart. It was funny how two people could be physically identical and yet have such contrasting personalities. It wasn't that Roxie thought Milly was hard, not at all, but she seemed more able to fend for herself than Lila, as if she'd been the one born with the armour. Still, it was good that she'd come to the village and made up with Lila because Roxie knew that it would have been hard for Lila to keep such a big secret all those years. Lila wasn't a person who would be able to hide her past easily and the fact that she'd said nothing about Milly's existence to anyone showed how difficult it had been for her.

'I guess we should get these two home.' Fletcher gestured at the dogs.

'They're both worn out, poor babies. What time's the minibus coming?'

Fletcher checked his watch. 'Half an hour.'

'Enough time to say goodbyes then scoop up Lila and Ethan and get them home. Lila must be shattered.'

Fletcher knelt down, picked up Glenda and handed her to Roxie then he picked up Stinky and they went to say their goodbyes.

EPILOGUE - LILA

'*A*re you sure you'll be all right today?' Ethan asked as he stood up and picked up his mug from the table.

Lila nodded. 'I'll be fine. It's a lovely sunny day, I have a good book to finish, a crochet project to start and two cats for company.'

'I've got my mobile volume right up, so anything you need, phone me and I'll get it for you.'

'Ethan you are wonderful, but you don't have to worry so much. I'm pregnant not ill.'

'I know that but with only six weeks left until the big day, I do worry. Plus, the midwife said you could go into labour before that, give or take a few days so—'

'Stop worrying!' Lila laughed. 'It will all be fine.'

She was sitting on one of their patio chairs with her feet up on another. On the table next to her was a tall glass of lemonade, her e-reader, crochet basket and mobile phone. Cleo and Willy were stretched out on the grass enjoying the sunshine. It was just before nine and Ethan was off to work on the cottage renovation which was coming along nicely. Lila knew he was anxious about getting it done before the baby arrived so he could take two weeks of paternity leave, but he was also anxious about leaving her alone.

'I know. I just can't help worrying about you both.' He placed a hand on her belly and she covered it with hers.

'We're fine. I promise you I won't do anything more taxing than a bit of crochet and I won't even have to make lunch because your mum's coming round with a picnic.'

'That's nice of her.'

'Your mum is an angel and she spoils me rotten.'

Lila's cheeks flushed as she said the words out loud. Freda had become like a mum to her, been even more caring since Lila and Ethan got married a month ago and Lila knew she'd make a brilliant grandmother.

'You deserve to be spoilt rotten.'

'Thank you. Now hadn't you better be going?' She winked at him. 'Not that I'm keen for you to leave, of course, but because the sooner you get there, the sooner the work will be done and you'll be able to come home.'

'I was thinking I could make us pizza for dinner.'

'Sounds good to me, but I'll do it.'

'You need to rest.'

'There's no way you're coming home after a full day of work and cooking for us both. I'm perfectly capable of making dinner.'

'Or we could order a delivery.'

Lila laughed. 'Whatever. Let's see how we feel later.'

'Okay.' He smiled then bent over and kissed her softly. 'And don't forget …'

'I'll phone if I need you.'

Lila sat back on the chair and closed her eyes. The breeze was warm, the chair soft and comfortable and the baby was particularly active this morning. She hadn't slept very well but knew she'd be able to catch up today and the advantage of a restless night was that she could catch up with her reading. The new e-reader that Ethan had bought her as a wedding present was backlit so she could read in bed without disturbing him. The getting up to use the toilet, for drinks and antacid, she couldn't help, but she always did her best to be as quiet as possible. It wouldn't be long and their nights would be disturbed by another person anyway, so Lila had wondered if the sleepless nights of later pregnancy were her body's way of preparing her for what was to come.

Tomorrow would be the one-month anniversary of their wedding and Lila had plans to make a special dinner and she'd ordered Ethan a gift to celebrate. It was just a keyring with one of their wedding photos on but something she knew he'd appreciate. It was one of their favourite photos from the wedding that someone had taken on their mobile and sent to them via email. Lila and Ethan had been dancing and laughing and the photo caught them like that, arms around each other, heads back, eyes locked. It summed up exactly how Lila felt about Ethan and how she thought of their relationship. She wanted them to have years of laughter, dancing and love ahead and believed that they would.

The baby wriggled and her belly went into a point under her fitted black maternity vest. She touched her hand to what looked like a small foot pushing against her skin, picturing the baby stretching its limbs. Some days, she wished they'd found out if they were having a boy or a girl at their last scan, and others she was glad they'd decided to wait because the surprise would be special.

Her mobile buzzed so she looked at the screen. It was a text from Joanne asking if she wanted anything from the café because she had a break at eleven, so Lila replied asking for an decaff iced tea and a scone. Joanne was no doubt bursting with news about the cottage she was buying with Max, and she kept bringing Lila catalogues of the things she wanted to buy for her new home when it was ready. Her excitement was infectious, and Lila planned on making some cushions and throws for Joanne when she got a chance so she could gift them to her as a house-warming.

More than ever, Lila was grateful for her friends. They kept in touch on a daily basis and she often saw Roxie or Joanne or both of them every day. She hoped they'd be around as much once the baby arrived because she had a feeling she was going to need their support as she navigated her way through motherhood for the first time.

Milly had also stayed true to her word and maintained regular contact. She'd been in Barcelona the week following the wedding, then Malaga and this week she was in San Diego. Lila would find that much travelling exhausting and unsettling, but her sister seemed to thrive on it. They'd always been different in that way, Lila longing for a base, a home of her own, and Milly yearning to see foreign shores. Perhaps they'd have been this way even if they'd had caring parents, but Lila suspected it had something to do with their childhood and that it had left its mark on them both. However, speaking to Milly about things over recent weeks as they Facetimed and Zoomed had been quite therapeutic, and it made Lila feel less isolated about her feelings and less guilty at how she'd handled things. There was no judgement from Milly because she'd been there and been through it too and sometimes Lila didn't even need to say the words because Milly just knew.

Life was like an ongoing lesson. Lila felt that she was constantly learning and adapting and the most important lesson she could take away from her childhood was how to be a better parent than her own had been. This baby would be loved, feel secure, never be humiliated or rejected and would always have a home to return to, even when he or she was grown-up. Lila and Ethan would spend time with their child, teach him or her right from wrong, and they would laugh together. A lot.

In the last year, Lila's life had changed beyond recognition. Despite what she'd thought after Ben had broken her heart, life had much to offer and it could be very good indeed.

Moving to Sunflower Street had been the best decision she'd ever made as she'd not only found her true love in Ethan but she'd also found her family.

THE END

DEAR READER

Thank you so much for reading *A Wedding on Sunflower Street.* I hope you enjoyed reading it as much as I enjoyed writing it.

I would be very grateful if you could leave a rating and a short review so I know what you enjoyed about the story.

If you'd like to connect with me, you can find me on Twitter **@authorRG,** on Facebook at **Rachel Griffiths Author** and on Instagram at **rachelgriffithsauthor** to find out more about my books and what I'll be working on next.

With love,
Rachel X

ACKNOWLEDGMENTS

Firstly, thanks to my gorgeous family. I love you so much! XXX

To my friends, for your support, advice and encouragement and to everyone who has interacted with me on social media, huge heartfelt thanks.

To everyone who buys, reads and reviews this book, thank you.

ABOUT THE AUTHOR

Rachel Griffiths is an author, wife, mother, Earl Grey tea drinker, gin enthusiast, dog walker and fan of the afternoon nap. She loves to read, write and spend time with her family.

ALSO BY RACHEL GRIFFITHS

CWTCH COVE SERIES

CHRISTMAS AT CWTCH COVE

WINTER WISHES AT CWTCH COVE

MISTLETOE KISSES AT CWTCH COVE

THE COTTAGE AT CWTCH COVE

THE CAFÉ AT CWTCH COVE

CAKE AND CONFETTI AT CWTCH COVE

A NEW ARRIVAL AT CWTCH COVE

THE COSY COTTAGE CAFÉ SERIES

SUMMER AT THE COSY COTTAGE CAFÉ

AUTUMN AT THE COSY COTTAGE CAFÉ

WINTER AT THE COSY COTTAGE CAFÉ

SPRING AT THE COSY COTTAGE CAFÉ

A WEDDING AT THE COSY COTTAGE CAFÉ

A YEAR AT THE COSY COTTAGE CAFÉ (THE COMPLETE SERIES)

THE LITTLE CORNISH GIFT SHOP SERIES

CHRISTMAS AT THE LITTLE CORNISH GIFT SHOP

SPRING AT THE LITTLE CORNISH GIFT SHOP

SUMMER AT THE LITTLE CORNISH GIFT SHOP

THE LITTLE CORNISH GIFT SHOP (THE COMPLETE SERIES)

SUNFLOWER STREET SERIES

SPRING SHOOTS ON SUNFLOWER STREET

SUMMER DAYS ON SUNFLOWER STREET

AUTUMN SPICE ON SUNFLOWER STREET

CHRISTMAS WISHES ON SUNFLOWER STREET

A WEDDING ON SUNFLOWER STREET

A NEW BABY ON SUNFLOWER STREET

NEW BEGINNINGS ON SUNFLOWER STREET

SNOWFLAKES AND CHRISTMAS CAKES ON SUNFLOWER STREET

A YEAR ON SUNFLOWER STREET (SUNFLOWER STREET BOOKS 1-4)

THE COSY COTTAGE ON SUNFLOWER STREET

SNOWED IN ON SUNFLOWER STREET

SPRINGTIME SURPRISES ON SUNFLOWER STREET

AUTUMN DREAMS ON SUNFLOWER STREET

A CHRISTMAS TO REMEMBER ON SUNFLOWER STREET

STANDALONE STORIES

CHRISTMAS AT THE LITTLE COTTAGE BY THE SEA

THE WEDDING

Printed in Great Britain
by Amazon